MEMOIRS
OF THE
DAMNED

YASIR HAYAT

Matador
9 Priory Business Park,
Wistow Road, Kibworth Beauchamp,
Leicestershire. LE8 0RX
Tel: (+44) 116 279 2299
Fax: (+44) 116 279 2277
Email: books@troubador.co.uk
Web: www.troubador.co.uk/matador

ISBN 9781780883410

British Library Cataloguing in Publication Data.
A catalogue record for this book is available from the British Library.

Typeset by Troubador Publishing Ltd, Leicester, UK

Matador is an imprint of Troubador Publishing Ltd

Printed and bound in the UK by TJ International, Padstow, Cornwall

First and foremost a huge thank you to my mum. I wasn't the best of children, but you were the best of parents.

To my darling siblings who shielded me from most of the world's woes. I don't know where I'd be without you.

To my dear friends Haris, Haseeb, Abdur Raheem, Ammar and Amin. Thank you for all your support, inspiration and for having faith in me, even when I had lost faith in myself.

Thank you to the Troubador-Matador team for helping me realise my dream and making it into a reality.

Above all else I thank Almighty God for the insurmountable blessings bestowed upon me. No amount of gratitude I can give is ever enough.

Finally, thanks to whoever you are, reader. This is for you so I hope you enjoy it.

Yasir Hayat

These foul rags I wear smell as bad as the ground I sit on saturated with blood. I can hear the groans of agony whistling on the wind. Soldiers picking up their comrades or what is left of them. Tentative eyes searching for fallen brothers, though my eyes long to see the departed. The near future is unclear because of my haunting past, this is how I came to know my tragedy began before I was even born.

DAMNATION

Mother was found in a pool of blood after giving birth to me. The law authority then, simple minded dogs, never took into account that it was her blood and not someone's she'd allegedly killed. They found her with two skewer shaped holes in her neck and deduced that she had got injured when she attacked someone being used in a ritual sacrifice to bring about my birth quicker in order to appease Satan. What feeble fools and what complete injustice did my family fall folly to. They hung her from the gallows barely after my birth. My father's story is a sorry one itself; sent to fight in a war that he did not believe in for king and country. He was killed in the line of duty apparently leaving us to fend for ourselves, or so I was told by the slave drivers. You must find it amusing how grim it all started. And so I was sent off to a children's workhouse.

Bizarre occurrences were rampant in my childhood. Always getting into fights with other child workers but it was as though I was immune to all the violence. The toughest of workers I turned into whimpering cowards. Daylight used to irritate my skin causing it to burst out with boils and no matter what amount of water I drank I was always thirsty. Every day was a struggle between the fights and the beating given to me by the slave drivers, who always took pleasure in telling me the demise of my parents. They were the dignitaries who instigated everything, the epitome of insult to injury. Enough was enough and I decided to run away. I ran and hid in a rich man's carriage hoping I could escape my nightmare or perhaps get somewhere far enough where I could end my life in peace. But the world began to smile upon me, finally.

The owner of the carriage was a wealthy gentlemen and he found me shivering in the luggage case. He took pity upon me and that pity turned into love over time. He saw a cold, hungry stowaway and brought me up as his own. Years passed in this tranquillity and my beloved benefactor married me off to his beautiful daughter Alisha. On our wedding night that sweet man died of heart failure. My beautiful wife followed a week after our union suffering from the plague. It was just me and Alisha's baby sister, Elisabeth left in this unforgiving world.

On Alisha's burial day I decided to drown my insurmountable sorrows in a sea of booze. As I lazily stumbled my way home I could swear I was being followed. Paralytic as I was, I had always had a heightened sense of awareness and this presence was far different than I had ever known; somewhat familiar as one knows oneself.

I was right, I was being followed by a wicked beast that jumped out of the bush and knocked me into the nearby stream. I had my skull smashed against the gravel next to the water bed for what seemed to me as an eternity. Before I completely blanked out of consciousness a dark figure hovered over me and this voracious beast. He was a tall man wearing a long black cloak with silk underlining, my death was about to begin. The man commanded the abomination;

"Cease, Emmanuelle!"

"Yes, Master."

The beast disappeared like a wisp of air; I crawled out onto the grass on my chiselled elbows, breathing heavily.

"Thank you, sir."

"Rise child, tell me your name."

I shakily stood up and took a long hard look at this man. He was wearing long black pants with leather frills down the side. He had a long black cloak and a sickly pale face hidden behind a bandana he wore over his mouth. To complete the picture he wore a strangely styled hat. His eyes, however, looked most menacing of all. They were not human eyes, they couldn't be. Orange pupils with blue irises and it looked as though his eyeballs pulsated within their sockets. I replied to his question:

"Andross Ameliyo, and you good sir?"

"You may call me Master Sereigravo."

"That thing before, it was a vampire. Am I right?

How did you get him off me?"

"Very perceptive, he is my pupil as I want you to be. Poor child, you have suffered many hardships in your life have you not? So I think it's appropriate that you get some much deserved recompense. I give you a choice, Andross, to live my kind of life as a detested vampire, eternal life without suffering to drink from the necks of humans in an endeavour to become more or…"

I waited on his every word, I was transfixed by his bulbous eyes as if I were in a trance.

"…you can turn around and walk away but if you do, you will not live to see another day, not another dawn. No flowery meadow or brisk air will ever caress your skin. Make your choice Andross! Choose."

I was offered death as a means to carry on existing. I had lived my life like a shadow. Like a candle's flame flickering in the wind, I decided that if I was to be damned in life it makes no difference that some mischievous sprite wants to devour my soul. I told him in a clear voice:

"Give me your death, I was dead in the first place."

Sereigravo began to chuckle to himself, his laughter escalated. He arched back and shrieked at the top of his stagnant lungs, and as if by magic there was a thunderous downpour that berated both of us, however he was not fazed in the slightest. As lightning struck the earth between us, Sereigravo vanished. A clap of thunder exploded above my head scaring me to my bones. I ran, as fast I could in my drunken state, away from this madness in the violent monsoon. In the disgusting mud I could see images, phantom apparitions that began to follow me no matter where I went. I tripped on a branch and fell face first into some muck. I raised my head out from the filth and a faint voice whispered in my ear.

"Wise choice."

Before I could turn around to see who it was, I felt a surging pain on the back of my head and my eyes closed as I was knocked unconscious. My last thought was of Elizabeth, my little Liza.

I woke up groggy in the most strangest of places. The ceiling was of dizzying heights, marble covered pillars with golden coloured ridges. The bed I was in felt as though I was lying on a cloud with cotton covers and silk sheets. A strange perfume on the pillows wafted throughout the entire room. Clearly I was somewhere belonging to a wealthy extraordinaire who could afford pillows. I could not help but think it was the same man from before. Along with the perfume I could smell a stench, something vile and strong. I rose up slowly as I tried to find out where this smell was coming from and it was then when I made the discovery. I no longer had hands; sharpened claws welcomed me instead of fingers.

My God what has happened to me, I thought. Everything felt different, I pulled up my velvet shirt which revealed more abnormalities. My whole body had transformed into an armour plated shell. I ran over to the mirror to take a better look but to my horror, no reflection. I shrieked at this find so I ran over to the bed to grab the duvet; I went back to the mirror and shook the duvet in front of it. I could see the duvet shake but not me shaking it. I began to breathe heavily, almost so that I thought I would pass out; that is when I finally discovered the most horrifying find of all. I thought my heart would be racing considering my condition but as luck would have it, no heart beat. So it was done, what was discussed in the thundering night finally came to pass. I was now a fully fledged and transformed vampire with no real similarities to what could be known as human.

I pulled myself together to find out what was going on, I required answers so I explored where I was. I left the luxurious room and found a hallway lined with doors to other room. Paintings hung from the walls with expensive frames. Most were of the man I saw, the cloaked menace that gave me a choice that I was quickly regretting with every passing moment. I found a stairway with a beautiful carpet going all the way down. A strange noise was coming from the bottom, like music but more realistic than instruments and the timing was perfect, as if it were choreographed. I wearily walked to the bottom to find the source of the music. It was a strange contraption, a box with a large disc oscillating inside of it under a pin that made melodious 'ping' sounds. The music was projected out of a flower-shaped horn of sorts.

"Welcome to my humble abode, Andross," an echoing voice boomed from behind me. I turned to find him, sat there in a leather chair in a room covered in black curtains. It was Sereigravo looking at me with those piercing eyes, I could feel his sight peering into my soul as though he had some power over me.

"Don't stand there like a sore thumb, come and sit we have much to discuss."

I walked over to him slowly and sat on the chair adjacent to him; we began to talk.

BECOMING

Sereigravo had much to say, I sat there listening to him intently.

"My dear boy, it is so good to see you reborn, as it were, in this state. Believe me if my heart worked it would surely beat for you. You must have many queries to ask of me but in time they will answer themselves. Allow me to educate you on your new found life."

The man had hardly begun and I didn't want to hear anymore.

"We are vampires Andross, we are the reason men fear the night. Our quarry are all living things with a heartbeat that depend upon their blood. We drink their lives in order to progress in our own. We will do so in order to carry on existing. Prolonged deficit of blood may result in our untimely demise. You are a fledgling so I must tell you of a few hazards."

What I was told was mythological, the kind of nonsense you tell children in order to entertain or, more probably, to frighten.

"Sunlight is your nemesis until your ascension when you become a vampire lord. You will blow up into ash in its rays so it would be wise of you to stay indoors until sunset. Safeguard your heart, even though it does not work if someone were to penetrate the thick scales of your chest you will cease to be. Don't allow your neck to be compromised, decapitation limits us much."

His jest was no doubt as hollow as his own dead body.

"Your name Andross, I do not like it, it is unfitting of your new found kinship with me. I dub thee Crimson, the demonic assassin of redemption. Yes that is much better, whilst with me and my protégé you will begin to realise your place in the world."

Whilst his mouth was moving I began to phase out slightly, just to survey my new surroundings. I couldn't help but feel these lodgings were no more than an extravagant sepulchre.

"Although some avenues to what you knew in your previous life are now closed to you, it gives you more exciting objectives to aspire to. You will be Emmanuelle's aid, he will show you our ways. Emmanuelle!"

Sereigravo shrieked and in came that hideous brute who attacked me, only this time he didn't look as intimidating. Maybe my eyes had accustomed themselves to accept this foul creature as something I could relate to. Emmanuelle walked over to us both, he then looked over to Sereigravo kneeling down with his head lowered in submission.

"Our weaknesses are not for eternity so don't be afraid, Crimson, you will learn your capacity through time. Enough of this for now, you two are my devoted disciples and you will do my bidding, but more than that we are a family. We will strike fear into the heart of mankind and rule like kings that belong to the living world and the dead one."

My voice erupted of its own volition:

"Yes Master."

"Excellent, you are a fine addition to my brood. Emmanuelle please escort Crimson here to be clothed and fed. Our work has just begun."

Months passed under the supervision of these two ghouls, they taught me things I never thought possible. I became a manic fratricide of mankind. The new found powers, the ability of unnatural restoration of wounded flesh was immense. My skin was like armour plating, every day that went by meant my strengths and defences were augmented, I felt invincible. Many moons passed and I had become accustomed to this dead life of darkness. Every soul I ate and the gallons of blood that nourished me gave me the drive to continue and truly evolve with this evil gift.

One day, awakening from my slumber in the eerie confines of my shadowy room, I heard whispers involving my name; curiosity compelled me to investigate the conversation outside my chamber door. Sereigravo was discussing something with Emmanuelle when suddenly Sereigravo's gaze fell upon me as I peered through the gap of the door frame.

"Well if you're up then don't just stand there and stare, come over here I have a task for you two."

I approached the two and Sereigravo continued.

"I want you to do something for me, there is a building not too far from here that belongs to a certain religious order of sort, and I wish for this order to not be there. Rather I want chaos and carnage, I want murder and mayhem to rule. I want blood to flow from the battered and mutilated faces and I want the last images these people see to be that of horror. I want you to destroy all the worshippers there."

Emmanuelle and I made haste, we came to that building at the edge of town and something caught my attention in the corner of my eye. As I stopped to focus my gaze Emmanuelle grabbed the scruff of my collar and threw me to the roof of an opposite building from our target, before leaping over and landing feet first, mere inches from my face. I looked up in slight distress and Emmanuelle peered down at me.

"We are not here to enjoy the sights, now on your feet, we must make ready."

We both crawled slowly to the edge of the roof and began scouting the building. Heavy fortifications were on the windows and the barbed chains on the spiked gates looked menacing. Armoured knights were patrolling the grounds, as if there was something of great importance within this building. The only way in was through the front door, but to enter this way would mean disposing of those knights which in turn meant no room for subtlety. After little discussion Emmanuelle and I stormed the building, the knights were alerted but we made short work of them. We ripped their helmets off with one claw and then decapitated them with the other in one single movement. One guard tried to close the doors but Emmanuelle tore through the feeble barricade with a ferocious roar; I followed immediately. Inside we found what our Master was talking of. The worshippers were cowering on the far side of their pews, praying pitifully to their lord for help. I admit I found it quite funny that these fools thought they had a chance just so long as they stay as far away as possible from us two in a locked building. I smiled at Emmanuelle and he could not help but chuckle a little himself; it was time to feast.

I cannot remember properly how I felt that night, I do, however, remember the sounds. The wet guttural sound of blood drenched groans. The metal clanking of armour being decimated revealing the human chest cavity. Most memorable of all was the breaking of bones and sinew under the power of my claws and canines during the evisceration of these bumbling mortals. Indeed the melodic mayhem that resonated was truly memorable, that night in the shrine.

We both climbed to the top of the steeple after all the gorging we had done on human flesh. We decided to have a rest and watch the last part of the night. Emmanuelle took this opportunity to have a small conversation with me.

"The electric air tastes sweet this night, my brother."

He snarled as he looked at me. I just nodded at

what he said, "Master Sereigravo has many expectations of you, as do I."

"Indeed so brother, I will not let either of you down."

"Only time will tell of that, it is however good to see how you've morphed from a feeble pile of putrid puss to a fantastic animal of the night."

Clearly he had poor social skills. I wondered to myself if Master Sereigravo had turned him from a human or from a bat. Emmanuelle had many thoughts on his mind that night and in his cantankerous demeanour tried his best to annunciate.

"So how are you finding this unorthodox lifestyle, Crimson?"

"It's hard to explain as I cannot compare being dead or alive at the same time however, since my becoming, I have had many revelations about my new found purpose."

"You have an uncanny resemblance to someone of grave importance to our clan."

Intriguing I thought to myself so I asked my admiring fiend,

"Who?"

"Sire Alledantoro!"

That name always echoed throughout our keep, he was indeed a vampire of great importance and status. He was the forebearer of our brood but only Sereigravo knew the full story and why he wasn't there with us at that time.

Before I could quiz him further we heard screaming from down below. From the dilapidated building a priest came running out with his tattered clothes barely escaping the fire we had started, which had consumed the entire architecture. He was hysterical.

"You vile parasites!" he cried, with tears streaking down his soot-covered face.

"May God punish you for what you have done, may your enfeebled corpses rot in the lowest depths of Beelzebub's anus. This is a holy shrine your ungodly hands have defiled, you will never get away with this. I am a true believer and while there is an ounce of life left within me I will fight you. Just wait you devils, wait."

So we waited to see what torture this deluded man had in store for us; he was not able to see where we were as the smoke was very thick. He knew us well and knew we had not gone far, we were close enough to see the carnage and after he had observed the slaughter of his people he knew we would savour the experience. His big surprise was a caged dog, no bigger than a cat, in the corner of its confines barking away. The priest pried the cage door open but the dog did not move. The priest commanded the dog to come out but the dog had smelt the burning carcasses from within and wanted no part in the priest's plan.

What we hadn't anticipated was what happened next, the priest lost his temper and threw a bone at the dog hitting it on its nose. The dog did not like this to say the least, the miniature beast leapt out with its jaws wide open and it took a large fleshy bite out of the priest's calf muscle on his left leg. The priest shrieked in agony and attempted to shake and hit the dog off, but the dog's jaws were locked. All we could hear were the dog's growls and the priest's shrieks as they both symbiotically pirouetted together in an unorganised ballet. Emmanuelle and I laughed and laughed before the priest finally got a hold of a stick and prodded the dog in his eye. The dog whimpered and released his hold, allowing the priest to hurriedly limp his way towards the burning entrance but now he was trapped between a burning building and an embittered canine with a bloody eye socket, that is not to mention two demons from above. He was granted his reprieve for his suffering, although I would imagine he didn't see this coming. The giant symbol hanging above the entrance of the shrine began to creak, the nails that held it together had melted away and as the priest worriedly looked up the fixture came falling down and impaled him head to toe where he stood.

I looked over to Emmanuelle and he was fixated by the dog, as if he'd seen something of great endearment. The dog looked up and Emmanuelle looked down, together they stared at each other and growled.

"Crimson, just look at that fine beast. Through the thick smoke he stares at me as if he's calling to me. One beast to another, I cannot ignore his call, I wish to keep him as a pet."

The events of the night made me feel ostentatious:

"I stare at the moon while I howl out of tune.
The dark is menacing the street,
Below I can feel the heat.
Time passes and it is nearly noon."

"What does that mean?"
"Nothing."
We left everything and headed back to our crypt.

FORGOTTEN LOVE

As Emmanuelle and I leapt from roof to roof we saw the sun rising on the horizon. Emmanuelle shouted, "Make haste brother."

And then I saw it again, the glimpse of something that had caught my attention from before. I stopped and this time indulged my gaze despite Emmanuelle's virulent protesting. It was at a closer gaze that I realised why I was captivated, a woman was brushing her long luscious hair in front of a golden framed mirror. The strokes of her brushing were poetic and soft, in full agreement with the curls of her hair at the tips. I was lost for words, I had seen women as a human and even as a vampire but why was I so drawn to this one? Emmanuelle angrily seized a hold of my shoulder and, without thinking or any real exertion, I struck him with a force that sent him flying to the floor of the high building we were standing on. The noise disturbed the woman so I took flight, I flew down to help a furious Emmanuelle back to his feet before continuing home.

The following night after feeding, I saw my Master trying to contain the ever irritable Emmanuelle in the main lobby of our mansion. He was still in protest of last night's excursion.

"But Emmanuelle you threw him into the air first and besides it's not like it hurt you."

"We were on a mission! The sun was on the horizon! He is a vampire not a human! He struck me with intent of harm! And all for some woman?!"

He was almost inconsolable. Master Sereigravo dismissed Emmanuelle to his chambers before diverting his attention to me. I was not expecting his mood.

"My dear Crimson, please sit with me, is what my snivelling disciple saying true?"

"Yes my Master, everything but the intent of harm. I don't know what came over me."

"I do."

Sereigravo began one of his speeches.

"You see, my boy, it is natural to sense things. Even though we are not of this world anymore we were once and the pleasures of the past life will never leave us. You must have smelt the pheromones coming from her extravagant hair and judging by your infatuation, the degree of enthusiasm of striking Emmanuelle effortlessly leads me to believe that she is indeed a thing of beauty."

Sereigravo almost sounded human.

"She will never be attracted to you as your appearance to your brethren is acceptable but to her and her kind is too fierce. I know how it feels to pursue something one cannot have but I will not hinder you. If you wish to indulge in this guilty pleasure then you have my full permission."

I wondered briefly as to why he was so forthcoming but it passed as I could not wait to see her again. Before I left, Sereigravo had one more thing to say.

"Crimson you have always been wise, you possess far more wisdom than me to know that to fully appreciate the beauty of a wild bird is to allow it to remain wild."

I pondered little on his cryptic advice and flew towards my destination.

I arrived at this unknown woman's house; I scaled the walls of an adjacent building so I could look into her window. I saw her sleeping this time and felt as though I could breathe again, despite not having the need for oxygen. The more I looked the closer I wanted to be near her, every breath she took was rhythmic and soft. This woman's complexion was pale and her face was symmetrical, almost perfect and lovely. I whispered to her as she slept:

"Oh sweet dame, who are you sweet thing?
This beauty of yours is truly worth cherishing.
I look at you and I am enthralled,
I whisper to you, this night I called.
Sitting here looking at you I am at peace,
You are magical like the myth of the Golden Fleece.
Indeed of your loveliness how much can I say?
It is as vibrant as a warm spring day.
I seek you out every time I wake,
The feeling of desolation is like being impaled by a thousand stakes.

This bewitching sensation is of such a sweet surrender,
The thought of losing you would split my heart asunder.
But for now my love, I pray thee to sleep,
Rest now because my feelings for you will forever run deep."

My gaze was fully sated and I decided to head back to the retreat. I visited her many times but dared not go near her window. Sometimes she would be asleep and I would whisper to her from afar or she would be brushing her hair. No matter what she was doing she looked beautiful doing it. I soon discovered she had a gentleman friend that would visit her once a fortnight to take her to dine at night; on one of these outings I followed them. They rode to an extravagant house in their horse and carriage, he would hold her silk gloved hand to help her down from the retractable stairs. They would eat and laugh their way merrily deep into the night, up until the establishment would close. He was indeed a charismatic persona that made sure her every need was attended to; he was entertaining and charming. He was fully aware of the wooing process and was well versed in flirtatious speech, he was truly an ideal suitor and if I was still alive he would have been my opposition.

The thought had crossed my mind, *what if I just killed him? She would be left all to me but then the happiness he gives her would be taken away. A double-edged sword or perhaps if I just removed myself from the equation, what need is there for me to be present other than my own desire?*

I had no idea what to do so I went back to my residence to ponder, I sat in my room for hours. Her face haunted me, *can I let go now that I am almost infatuated with her or can I do the unspeakable? Do I make her my soul mate forever and ever?* I stormed out of the mansion at night, wilful to carry out the dark deed. As I left I saw Master Sereigravo sat in front of a painting of a woman.

"My forgotten love was not meant to be caged so all I can do is sit on its egg."

His cryptic jabbering was of no consequence to me at the time so I flew, house to house, until my quarry was finally present. I entered her window and crept slowly to her bedside, slowly kneeling down to take a look at her closer than I had done ever before. Her radiance was profound and I was dumbfounded by her.

"Hello."

She spoke suddenly, startling me so that I jumped back with such a force that I accidentally broke her bookcase. She began to laugh.

"I'm sorry did I frighten you?"

"Do you always greet men who creep into your room with such a smile?"

Her laughter carried on, it wasn't loud it just lasted slightly longer than last time, she had a chirping laugh like a bird's tweet. So fresh and comforting her presence was to me.

"Men do not dare enter my premises as I am royalty, commoners do not have permission and you are no man."

"So you know I am not of this world, and you are not afraid of what I could do to your fragility?"

She angled her face slightly whilst still looking at me and her smile grew.

"Why would you want to do anything to me? Considering the effort you've been through just so you could see me every night."

I had no reply to her so I just paced her room slowly, not even looking at her. I regained my composure and asked, "How do you know I visit you at night?"

"I felt you, every night whilst I slept I could feel someone watching me, a mysterious presence looking at me with admiration."

I looked at her and she did not flinch despite the fact that I was probably the most formidable sight she had ever seen.

"I am a vampire young miss, I dream of you with my waking eyes. I am fully intoxicated by your femininity, I am drunk on your beauty and I want you to be mine forever. The only way for this to be is to make you into my soul mate."

I have no idea why I was speaking like that to her, furthermore I didn't expect her reply.

"So you are in love with me and insistent on destroying me, you wish to spoil me yet it was my grace that attracted you to begin with. If your face is anything to go by I will lose my beauty instantly, but I will not stop you."

She revealed her silky skinned neck with her veins calling out to be drained. I walked up to her with a scowl and with conviction, and she did not care in the slightest. I leant over to bite and my lips were touching her neck before I stopped. I realised something right at the moment, Sereigravo had said something about wild birds:

"Beauty is not to be caged."

"What does that mean?" she asked.

I was completely ashamed with myself, how could I behave such a way with something so precious. I stormed off.

"You are leaving without introducing yourself, how rude," the woman said.

"You speak to me as if you speak to a suitor, like I am an ordinary person but more than that. Your mannerism towards me is that of attraction, why?"

"Because sir, the thought of losing you would split my heart asunder."

She had heard my words but better yet, she was wooed by those words.

"You heard my heart's praise?"

She flirtatiously walked over to me and put her supple hand on my chest, slowly caressing my shoulders as she walked round me and said, "You are the guardian of my dreams, the only reason I go into a magical stupor and indeed I am in love with you as we speak. I feel the love coming from you, I know you cannot hurt me or change me."

"If you love me then what of your gentleman friend that visits fortnightly?"

"He is my confidant, my royal aide that does the provisions route for me. A mere peasant hired by my family."

With excitement I took hold of her and held her,

enclosing her within my arms, she buried her face in my chest as though it was a comforting pillow.

"I have longed for you so."

She was silent, just at peace being so close to me. She raised her gaze and looked deep into my sorrowful eyes, this time she was not expecting what I had to say.

"I am never going to see you again."

"Why?"

I developed a bulge in my throat.

"I was completely adamant that you were to transform for me but now that I have seen that a wild bird must remain wild, I am truly ashamed of myself."

Her gaze was no longer on me as she backed away.

"You are going to leave my life?"

"How well do we know each other? To be with me would be to never see the sun the same again, to know voracious hunger more than you've ever known before."

Every word that came out of my mouth hurt her.

"Do you know what blood tastes like? It is warm and thick, like a viscous formula full of decay seeping into your throat. Its taste lingers, like a corpse in your mouth and before long it turns into ash. After a while you are required to hollow out the coagulated residue from your throat with a sharp instrument. I do not believe that is what you want? Your beauty will subside and I will never have that."

We stood silently looking at each other's feet, not knowing what to say. After a while she took a deep breath and said, "I understand but know that I will always keep an eye out for you in the corner of my eye, and my ears will always yearn for your song."

A tear trickled down her valuable face, as it fell from her chin I reached out with my claw and it splashed on my palm. She looked down to see me clench it hard in my fist.

"Every part of you must be kept in high adoration, even your sorrow."

This brought a slight smile to her chaste face, I left without saying goodbye and I didn't look back. Back in the crypt I was greeted by a welcoming Sereigravo.

"You've come back and it seems alone."

"Indeed, beauty is not meant to be in a cage and she was not in my destiny."

"It's OK to feel this way, do not be ashamed."

I was too upset to reply and resided myself mournfully to my chambers. How cruel fate can be; I said farewell in my heart to my fair mistress who had resembled my lost Alisha so remarkably.

MADNESS

Isolation can drive many to madness, however desolation can kill a man. I have delved into all levels many times in both incarnations. It's not a matter of circumstance per se but rather of what you allow to happen with what you are given. If the opportune moment is readily forfeited due to whatever reason, then you must abide by its consequence. I broke off from reality for a long while, my heart could not take going on anymore. Despite the countless visits from my accomplice and Master, I could not move. My chambers had become my living tomb, nothing made sense to me anymore. It is an imbalance in the universal fabric that I should be tormented for such a long period of time with little or no recourse. My lack of appetite brought about by my depression resulted into rigor mortis.

It got so bad that even blinking became an arduous undertaking and my mouth laid open. The sorrows from my past haunted me, from the taunts in the workhouse to the beautiful embodiment of femininity I left behind. I prayed for hell to swallow me whole, I wasn't that far off anyway. In the final moments before evaporating I peered towards the floor, I saw a rat looking for food. It must have smelt my foul odour coupled with my rotting flesh and came to investigate. It crawled up my leg and sought to eat the only part of me that retained any tenderness, my tongue. At this most wretched moment I had an epiphany; as soon as the vermin bit upon my tongue I bit down hard into its spine and its blood gushed onto every contour of my mouth.

The blood from this creature was just enough for me to get some movement. I waddled over to the staircase, like a haemorrhoid inflicted gorilla. In my condition, walking with finesse was out of the question, so instead of devising a plan to descend down the staircase with elegance, I merely leant forward and fell down them. The thud attracted a curious Emmanuelle and a very happy Sereigravo to me.

Sereigravo knelt down and said, "May I assist you, my dear boy?"

"Yes Master, may I have some blood?"

Once I was back to full health, Master Sereigravo quizzed me as to what was going on with me. I informed him of my epiphany, in the madness I found myself engulfed in, I came to realise that I am a vampire. I am an affliction upon the living world that cannot die by natural means. I am devoid of any real humanity and to indulge in love or compassion would be futile and against my nature. Sereigravo had mixed feelings about my sudden realisation yet he said nothing, instead he had a strange look on his face. I wasn't seeking his approval, I wanted to kill. I wanted to hunt the living, to devour innocence. All I wanted to do at this moment in time was to rip out the world's throat and writhe in its innards. I had the most extravagant macabre desire to consume existence, I wanted to become the personification of hell. I no longer cared for the intricacies of the mortal coil, what need was there now as I had ascended into becoming a vampire lord? I reached such maniacal heights in my exploits that even Emmanuelle avoided me in our lair. I was undeterred, every night I would hunt and kill without remorse. I did not care for protests or limits, my savagery was destructive.

In my blood-drunk state I would ritualistically leave the crypt with the unbridled desire to cause malice and horror. I did not do it because I felt any sort of pleasure out of it, I had no feelings. I did what pleased me because it was what I was meant to do. Upon returning back to my home one night, I heard a voice coming from a distance as I walked lonely through a quiet district in the dead of the night. I followed the voice through an alleyway and into a quiet enclosed area with a well. Next to the well was the source of the voice: a small man with a scraggy beard and dishevelled hair, who was rocking himself jabbering something incoherent. His clothes were in tatters and from him emanated an ungodly smell.

"Don't step on that bird!"

I was slightly taken aback by this shabby little person resembling a rodent. There was no bird, what was he speaking about?

"Don't step on him!" He cried again before looking at the starry night and continuing, "Birds don't like to be stepped on and they like to fly. They want to fly in the sky above our heads. They like to sing, to talk to each other. They like to go 'purr purr' and to lay eggs. Don't you dare step on him!"

I was confused to say the least but my curiosity towards this man's enfeebled state of mind forced me to humour his delusions.

"Well sir, if you describe him to me, I will be sure to not step on him."

"Oh come on are you crazy?! Why do you want me to describe him to you? He's right in front of you, open your eyes!"

I was so intrigued by his madness that I decided to play along. I wearily avoided the imaginary bird under his manic gaze and I sat next to him as he rocked away. I wanted to find out this man's story so I began to converse with him.

"I hope you don't think of me as being intrusive, sir, but who are you?"

"Intrusive? Only intrusive are those intruders that intrude an interlude, I don't like intruders."

I could sense this becoming a long night so I simply said, "Please tell me about yourself."

"The intruder asking intrusive questions, somehow irony just doesn't cut it. I don't belong here you think, you know it all but you don't. I am not happy here, in the world in this form. I am so brittle in a harsh environment. How we survived as humans for so long is beyond me but I recognise the purpose."

Like with most of the things I got myself into, I began to tire of him quickly.

"Having said that I am still unhappy, this life, this existence is not what I wanted and I didn't even have a choice in the matter. It's too hot or cold, it's too hard or soft. It's never what I want. In the unlikely event of me attaining something I require it doesn't last but when there is something inhibiting me then that always lasts."

His speech, although ambiguous beyond compare, resembled something I could reflect upon. He continued;

"It makes me sick just how inconsistent this world is, where someone's pleasure is another's pain. And that's not even the real reason I don't like being here. Let's face it people are always going to be tyrannous regardless, it can't be helped. Get down from there Adam, right now!" he roared, looking at the area where he had first laid eyes on me. Perhaps he was speaking to his imaginary pet bird that I unknowingly almost stepped upon.

"Is Adam your pet bird, sir?"

"No! You bumbling buffoon, Adam is the squirrel that lives inside my head, now do you wish for me to continue or not?"

His rant was amazing; he was clueless to the world around him. I could not help but think what trauma this soul had endured to reduce him to such a ridiculous state. However my curiosity was not satisfied.

"Please forgive my impertinent behaviour, continue."

"I shall, as I was saying people, by nature are tyrannous and we are as such because we don't want to help it, we don't want to change for the best. I didn't want to come here, I was sent here that is why it hurts so much because I am not from here. I don't know anything really of that existence but of what I am told."

I was aware of a certain plague driving people insane in the area, at that time I deduced that it was this plague driving him mad.

"It had none of these negativities and, from what I know in perspective to this existence, at least there I was happy in some form. Even though I was shapeless I did exist, along with everyone else I had to be happy, this place is terrible."

Such a tongue of sanctimonious platitudes I was slightly in awe of his plight, which begged the question, *where did he come from*?

"So tell me, my dear philanthropist, where are you from then? A place or country?"

"Damn it you confounded fool, did I say I was from a place? I belonged to a religious order, I belonged to heaven, I was the knight of the east in the order of Heaven."

He was beyond anything salvageable, all that remained was the unmistakeable face of hysteria found in a dead dog. I could however relate to this man's misfortune. Like me he had lost everything he held dear, I had no idea of his so-called origins but his pain was palpable. I offered him a choice.

"I sympathise with you old man, and only because I do, I will give you a gift you would not have received on any other occasion."

The rabid cretin stared at me with bewilderment.

"I give you a choice to live my kind of life as a detested vampire; eternal life without suffering, to drink from the necks of humans in an endeavour to become more or…" Sereigravo's words were coming out of my mouth, "…you can turn around and walk away but if you do, you will not live to see another day, choose!"

There was an absent look on his face as though I told him his family had died, he stood up and took a long hard look at me, arched forward.

"You want me to join you, in a life of being damned?"

I did not respond but just continued to stare at him. He began to smile as though he had accepted, but this ingrate had other ideas. He began to, at first, slowly giggle, which then escalated to whole-hearted laughter. His euphoria got to such a state that he began rolling on the floor, slapping the cobbles as though he had heard the most preposterous thing in his life. His mockery of my offer was evident.

"When I first laid eyes on you I had a feeling you were stupid, but now I see your idiocy is irreversible. Do you think I am a mad man, mad enough to curse myself at your hands in this life and the next? No my good sir, you are the mad man. Adam! *purr* look *purr* he's mad."

His laughter continued after his condescending speech, he stood up and began to walk away. I did not feel angry at the mockery nor did I feel belittled. All I could think of was that even in his dementia ridden state he rejected immortality because he thought vampirism is wrong. In such a state to revile, my new found animation made me wonder *why did I not reject it and I was perfectly sane*? The feeling passed momentarily as I proceeded to fish out the bucket from the well and hit the old man on the back of the head with it.

As the wooden bucket hit his head it broke into kindling, sending him flying into a wall. Both blows contributed to the old man's unconsciousness. I waited until he regained his awareness only this time he was hanging upside down from one leg that I was holding, looking down a staggering height from the steeple top.

"You think this matters, my life was forfeited when I was thrown out of the order. You, however, are a walking curse, you have damned yourself so you shall never know peace, never!"

I took a hold of his head and pulled it towards my face so that our noses were almost touching, "Hear me well, old man, as this is the last thing you will hear. I don't care for your jabbering. If it is true what you say then I am left with only one option. I will take as many people down with me as I can."

I ripped out his clavicle bone, his pain ridden

screech was deafening so I relinquished my hold and allowed him to die.

Back in the crypt I pondered on my night's exploits, especially the madman. Sereigravo was about to retire to his chambers so I quickly took the opportunity to ask him a question.

"Master, please may I speak with you?"

"Oh of course, my child, you need not enquire just speak."

"I was out tonight and I came across a man who spoke of a religious order called Heaven and I was wondering if…"

Sereigravo dashed over and took a hold of me with brutal power, "What madness gave you information on the order of Heaven?"

"I just happened upon it Master I…"

Sereigravo pushed me away, he was in a great deal of mental anguish when I uttered the name of the religious order that the man belonged to.

"It may interest you to know that Sire Alledantoro was a member of the order of Heaven. He was to embark on a final ritual which would solidify his and our status among the hidden elite, but something went wrong. We were banished from the membership forever and never heard from our Sire again, we have been searching for him since so that any honour lost may be restored. Who told you of this? Where are they now?"

I lowered my gaze.

"He is dead now, Master."

Sereigravo was no longer happy to see me, he was in fact quite distraught.

"I assure you Master, he was in no condition to inform us of anything, his delusions were out of control."

"My dear Crimson, you may have destroyed any chance we had of getting back to our honour. I do not wish to look upon you anymore."

Sereigravo, the most maudlin I had ever seen him, turned away from me before closing his chamber door. I had never felt so dejected in my entire existence. I felt as though I had robbed Sereigravo of the one chance of glory to redeem our clan. The night was filled with bad omens.

DESTINY

The overwhelming sense of dread had crept into my thoughts, how could I have been so stupid? *It's no wonder my Master is worried by my ruthlessness,* I thought back then. When you become absent-minded then critical detail is no longer a factor for concern and it is to that fatal error that I fell folly.

I dared not leave my chambers in case my Master's disappointed gaze was to fall on me; what little provisions I had in my room were what I lived on for a few nights.

The following week an unlikely visitor knocked on my door. I thought perhaps I had been forgiven and Sereigravo was outside my bed chamber with a chalice of fresh blood as a sign of my guilt being forgiven. I was wrong however, as it was just the wretched Emmanuelle telling me that Sereigravo wished to charge us both with a very daring mission.

I saw this as an opportunity to atone for my fault and get back on Sereigravo's good side. I quickly met them both in the main lounge. Emmanuelle was standing there hunched forward as the reputable minion that he was, but Sereigravo had his chair facing the other way towards the fireplace, looking at a portrait of a woman. Clearly I wasn't out of the woods yet but I was eager to learn about what he wanted me to do.

"I wish to ascend, I feel as though my time has come. But before I do there is a ritual that needs to be completed, the spilling of virgin blood on a sacrificial altar. I need you to go and get a dignitary in a nearby castle. It will be treacherous, you may not make it back."

"I understand Master, come Emmanuelle we must go."

As I took a few steps I saw that Emmanuelle wasn't listening to me, before I could say another word Sereigravo spoke.

"Crimson, he will not be accompanying you, rather he will be there merely as a scout to inform me whether you were successful…or not."

I smiled as I understood exactly what Sereigravo meant. I had fallen so far from their graces that in order for me to remain a part of their brood I had to risk my immortality.

"Your will be done, my Master."

I had let my Master down to a point where he no longer cared if I was in his clan or a festering pile of ash. I had to atone for my monumental transgression by throwing myself into harm's way and into the whim of fate. When I finally arrived I saw why such a preposterous task was given to me. Even with Emmanuelle by my side this would be a suicidal endeavour. There were indeed dignitaries living here as I could see an extravagant castle.

However, much to my dismay, it looked as though this particular castle was situated in amongst an army barracks, the likes of which I had never seen. The entire locality was infested with knights as though they were locusts. Everyone looked formidable with spiked gauntlets and iron greaves. They had helmets the size of boulders, not to mention their vast array of horrific weaponry.

Claymores or broadswords were being carried by nearly everyone there. The arsenal was immense and got more and more daunting the more I looked. Flails, maces, war hammers and halberds were being distributed as though they were expecting something or someone. Lances and spears, not to mention the catapults and siege towers they had at their disposal, were being readied. *Master Sereigravo never wished for me to make it back, why else such a mission*? I was not about to admit defeat by any count.

I saw a route that took me directly into the castle grounds and far from these abysmal fortifications. The best way to navigate my way to the castle outer barricade was by stealth, so I decided to sneak my way there. When I could I would disguise myself as a soldier and make my way past tricky obstacles in plain sight of the enemy. Every nerve in my dead body was shot, I was having difficulty keeping my composure but if I was to be successful then I had to block out the dread.

Thankfully I made it to the outer barricade, I peered through the wooden gates to see that there were considerably less knights there but as luck would have it they were situated at every main entry point. These knights were slightly different, their weapons were light and refined and their armour was glistening in the moonlight. I could clearly tell that they were special guards. I was not fazed, I mustered the courage to lay waste to the castle's exterior, an alarm was sounded but it was already too late.

I was inside the main lobby of the castle, dismembering wave upon wave of knights. Every corridor lead to the one I was in, so it was hard to be ambushed, apart from the door behind me that I had barricaded with a halberd. I was shot at by crossbows and arrows, as I dodged these meagre projectiles a javelin flew at me and scathed my face slightly. I was cornered by forty knights and another hundred or so were breaking the door down from behind me. I used the javelin lodged in the wall to jump off and cleared my opponents in one leap.

I dashed up the stairs with a bloodthirsty mob in hot pursuit. Luckily I saw a humoungous statue midway up the staircase so I broke its foundation and hurled it at the knights. They toppled instantly under its weight and velocity, conveniently it had lodged itself against the lobby entrance door so no more reinforcements could come in and stop me from my task.

I had free reign over the dignitaries now, I followed the hallway and could smell unspoilt meat. I could hear whimpering coming from one of the rooms, so with a roar I kicked open the door and made my way in. I saw a petite young woman cowering on her bed, shivering with fear.

"You will come with me young miss, you have a meeting with destiny."

I preached to her with a sense of self-righteousness. She looked at me with her bloodshot eyes.

"Andross?"

I was bewildered.

"What did you say woman? How do you know such a name?"

She slowly rose to her knees whilst she was still on her bed and gazed lovingly towards me.

"Don't you recognise me?"

Her eyes had past recollection of sorrow. Her face had an unmistakeable resemblance to someone I had seen before, I felt drawn to her.

"What is this witchcraft? Who are you and how do you know me?"

She wept uncontrollably and raised her arms towards me, "It's me...Elizabeth."

Dear merciful God, could it be? Or had the years of torment in this wretched form finally taken its toll? My vision became blurry and my lips began to quiver; my limbs began to shake and a tear trickled down my face. I could barely utter a word.

"L...L... Liza?"

"Andross!"

She shrieked with her arms open and tears gushing forward. I leapt to her bedside and grabbed hold of her shoulders, we both gazed mournfully into each other's eyes. The insurmountable pain of losing her and being reunited with her under such circumstance was profound. I held her close as I did my undead life, my darling sister, the baby of my human family had returned to me. My sorrow echoed throughout the castle.

I kissed her cheek, brow and forehead before embracing her again, her anguish was as equal to her joy of seeing me again. We wept into each other's embrace and it seemed as though time had stopped. I had been given the one shred of decency back to me and felt reborn.

We both looked at each other and our tears had not subsided, finally we began to smile, locked in each other's gaze.

"Andross, where did you go?"

She started stroking my malevolent face and wiping my tears away. I held her hand softly in my claws and kissed her fingers. She saw my disfigured face and morphed hands.

"My darling sibling, what has happened to you?"

I was overcome with brotherly duty towards her.

"Despite my appearance you recognised me, after all these years?"

"When you disappeared Aunt Lucia took care of me, we looked everywhere for you but after a month the authorities stopped searching. We had thought you committed suicide or fled the country. Every night for the first two years I pined for you and kept a vigil. But even I gave up on you, token of my heart, even I gave up."

She lowered her gaze in sorrow as though I would be disappointed in her. I raised her chin and gave her an affectionate smile.

"My sweet sister, after all these years and looking the way I do, you were still able to recognise me. Flesh of my flesh, I would die a thousand times for your smile. You are the object of my sympathy and I love you."

I held her in my arms once more, the lobby door finally smashed open and a cadre of elite knights stormed the castle. A group of them wandered into my sister's room where they found us. I was now sat up in the bed cradling a silently blissful Elizabeth, who had now finally stopped crying.

"Release her fiend and I will promise you a merciful death devoid of torture."

Elizabeth looked up at the knight and got off the bed of her own accord.

"This man will come to no harm under this roof."

"But mistress, you do know he is a vampire?"

"Yes I know what he is, but do you know *who* he is?" she asked the confused assembly of knights. "He is the light bearer of the house of Marioss."

Marioss was the name of her father and my beloved benefactor. On hearing this, every knight fell into silent awe of me. They lowered their weapons, the hilt of every axe and tip of every sword was ceremoniously put on the floor. The knights sequentially kneeled in front of me with lowered heads.

Confused at this display, I looked over at Liza who was indicating with her eyes for me to look at a portrait hanging on the wall above her bed. It was a picture of a handsome young man, standing on a large marble stone. It was a commemoration portrait with a plaque that had a written inscription. It read:

'In loving memory of Andross Ameliyo, loving son, loving husband and loving brother to the house of Marioss. The light bearer of our family, may God rest his soul.'

I choked in sorrow at this picture, I looked tearfully at a happy Liza and nodded in agreement to her. Suddenly the windows smashed in, a large grey cloud flew in and knocked the knights out of the room. When the cloud rested, I saw that it was Emmanuelle who then proceeded to barricade the door. I took a hold of Liza and held her in the corner of the room, as Emmanuelle approached I shielded her from this abhorrent menace.

"What are you doing? Our Master is waiting and you are here reminiscing."

I looked over my shoulder at the mortified Liza and I stroked her shoulder to reassure her.

"Did he send me here to kill my only living relative?"

"He sent you here so you could become a true vampire lord and dispose of your human side."

I was not going to reason with him or debate the matter; brainless swine such as Emmanuelle are incapable of adhering to such understandings. This left but one option, I had to kill my un-dead brother. I clenched my claws together and looked Emmanuelle straight in his eyes. He began to snarl and raised his arms, we attacked each other in mid-air. We scratched each other's faces and gnawed away at each other's limbs. We continued to fight upside down standing on the ceiling, with a nauseous Elizabeth looking on. I was, however, no match for this evil agent, he took hold of my collar and catapulted me into the memorial portrait, I landed on the bed.

Emmanuelle landed on his feet and had his sights set on my beloved sister. I could not stand for this abomination to touch her. I picked up the remnant of the portrait that had fallen on me, and as Emmanuelle came within arm's distance of Liza I pelted him with the frame in the mouth. The impact of the blow sent him flying into the wall. Emmanuelle was bleeding from his mouth, at closer inspection he found one of his fangs were missing. The metal edge of the frame must have severed his canine, he was incensed at me. Luckily the elite knights came to save us, ten of them fought him off. Their movement was synchronised and each one of them looked like they had been in many wars. They had restrained the wretched beast but no amount of hacking or stabbing was penetrating his armoured shell. Emmanuelle began to break free from his bonds, I knew if I didn't do something he would kill all the knights with me and my sister included.

They might not have had the right arsenal to kill a vampire, but I did. I leapt into the air over the knights' heads and aimed straight from Emmanuelle's chest. I held my claws together in a cone shape and embedded it as deep and hard as I possibly could. Emmanuelle glared into my eyes; I could see desolation in his eyes and at that moment he disintegrated into ash. The knights that were holding the bonds fell to the floor and Liza came running and held me from behind. I turned to hold her in my arms.

"Everything's OK now, Liza."

"Light bearer, mistress, are you both OK? Are there anymore of these fiends?"

Elizabeth was silent and I shook my head at him. I held Liza's face so that she would look at me.

"My beautiful sister I must go and do one last errand."

As I walked away she grasped my wrist very hard with both hands, "Andross don't leave me, please!"

"For the safety of our family I go, if anything should happen to me know that I love you more than life itself. Don't spend your life as a shadow, live and be happy. I will do my best to come back to you as soon as I can."

I reassured her before leaving. Elizabeth fell to the floor and the knights consoled her, she was a strong soul and of my family. I had to kill Sereigravo. One of the knights showed me a faster way to get back to the castle through a neighbouring kingdom. I made haste to my nemesis.

RESPITE

I was intoxicated by revelation, Sereigravo had orchestrated a malicious ploy for me to destroy my own identity. He wanted me to hand over my human sister to him for completion in his ascension. The regret I had felt before for letting him down transformed to vengeance for this betrayal. I no longer cared about being the best vampire in his eyes. Before my stupidity took a hold of me I was in a loving family, even though I gave up on life at least one remaining member kept me in her heart. Her pining for me was incentive enough for me to make sure she should never come to any harm. I needed to make my way back to the mansion to confront the fork-tongued fiend, to make him confess and release him from existence.

I was making my way through a neighbouring kingdom and as I was running through a strange sort of nostalgia took hold. These walls and streets had a familiarity but I could not decipher when or where. The buildings and alley ways I somehow knew, in fact

I actually knew which street lead where but still did not know how. As I began to survey, a shiny piece of metal glistened in the corner of an alcove over a doorway. I stood over the metal piece and sat down to inspect it further. It looked as though it was a sharpened piece that you would find on an axe to counteract the weight. As I put it in my pocket I felt a surging pain in the back of my head. I lost consciousness.

I woke up groggy in strange surroundings, I was in a courtyard with fifty or more spectators and a noose around my neck. I was standing on some gallows with my hands tied behind my back. The crowd mocked and jeered before an elderly man, this entire night had been full of past demons being exercised. I began to feel paranoid as I felt as though I had seen this frail vagabond before too.

"Be witness oh people of this realm that God's justice is swift and righteous!"

The crowd cheered in agreement.

"Let no naysayer tell us how we deal out fairness, we are true believers!"

This man had the favour of the people but I wanted to know something from him.

"What is my crime?"

"Your crime is being an abomination onto the Lord, incidentally what name shall I inscribe on your coffin?"

I peered into his old and sagging eyes and said, "Andross Ameliyo."

The old man's face dropped, he was mortified at my name. He gasped to the crowd, "Witch boy! Witch boy!"

The crowd was in panic and before I could make sense of what was going on the signal was given to pull the gallows' lever. It seemed as though this entire kingdom was not aware of how to deal with unearthly menaces such as myself. I cut my bonds and the noose before confronting the crowd. The old man had been led away to safety along with three others to a nearby mansion. I was standing in front of thirty or so armed knights and the mortified crowd.

"Halt there fiend! Vampires have no calling to this world. You shall die!"

"Pitiful human look at me, I am already dead and you shall join me."

"Your feeble threats bear no gravity to me."

"Is that why I can hear your heart pounding away at your chest, just by you looking at this infernal cadaver of a warrior? In any case, I am your damnation."

I dashed over to him before I ripped off his helmet and snapped his head back with such a force that it looked towards the crowd whilst his body still faced me. The crowd was in upheaval, fleeing as fast as they could at these atrocious sights.

I bludgeoned, hacked and dismembered my way through the knights. One knight in particular was different, it looked as though he was bred for war. He impaled me with the halberd he was carrying and hoisted me into the air. Having just missed my heart I took revenge on him by showing him a little display of my own. With one claw I broke the head off the halberd and took it out of my chest with the other free claw. As

I fell to the floor I threw the shard into the knight's face, rendering his head in two. As his corpse fell to the ground the remaining knights fled in terror.

I seized hold of one of them and quizzed him, "The old man from before, who is he?"

"He...he's a dignitary, he and his partners own a workhouse nearby. They've owned it for decades, please spare me."

The root of my pain originates here, no wonder this place looks familiar. Those men are the slave drivers and the ones who had my mother killed. I ran to the mansion and tore down the door, in the main hall they were being protected by more knights. I took out a souvenir from inside my cloak and rolled it over to them. It was the severed head of the knight with the shard still stuck in, the one who thought it was a good idea to skewer me with a halberd. The knights wanted no part of this and abandoned their enfeebled charges.

"You cried, 'Witch boy' old man," I said, pointing at the man from the gallows with three others huddled in fear behind him. "Why would you say such a thing?"

"We hung a witch decades ago, you're her son we put in the workhouse to absolve her sins."

He remembered me with a precise memory. It wasn't enough that they killed my mother for evil reasons, it wasn't enough I was taunted for most of my childhood. The thing that infuriated me most was that they still thought they did the right thing. They still believed with such fervour that an innocent woman deserved such a severe penalty and then, as a favour to her soul, her son was made a slave to serve penance. I was thoroughly going to enjoy this. I remembered everything they used to taunt me with, every hurtful word and action.

For the speaker out of the four, I grabbed him by his mouth and ripped out his tongue so that he would never harm anyone from lying with it again. The speaker had collapsed from the pain and I proceeded to remove his lower jaw from his skull. As the life passed from his scabrous body, the speaker's friends began to flee. I threw the removed jaw at conspirators as they wearily ran away. The jaw hit the one in the middle and he fell to the floor. The remaining two deserted my new victim, as he got up I was standing in front of him. I seized hold of his collar.

"So which one are you?"

He looked like the one who told me how he slapped my mother when she pleaded her innocence.

"Were you the one who struck my mother with an open hand?"

I wasn't waiting for an answer, I held both of his arms and with one hefty kick sent him flying into the nearby wall. His arms remained in my possession, no longer would they harm any innocent and he died upon impact in a *pool of his own blood,* just as they found my mother.

The two that remained had fled in opposite directions but I could smell their fear. I took flight and brought both of them back to the courtyard that I had left littered with bodies. I threw them both on the dismembered carcasses. One stood up and lowered his head as I approached.

"So which one are you?"

"He pulled the lever to the gallows!" The other heretic spoke instead, *what he was hoping for by telling me this* I don't know but I redirected my gaze to the new found advocate.

"So that would make you which one?"

He looked like the one that was a supposed eye-witness. He began stammering, his punishment seemed fitting. I hollowed out his eyes, as he writhed in pain I punctured his chest and severed his aorta. I retracted my claw from his rib cage and from his chest shot out a six foot jet of arterial blood which splattered into the night sky. I made my way over to the remaining member who was still standing in the same place, motionless.

"I remember you now old man, out of the four you were the only one who treated me right."

He nodded his head silently.

"Yet you are still the one who dropped her from the gallows, why?!"

"I had no choice, I followed orders, that's all."

"An innocent mother died at your hands because you were following orders!"

He had nothing to say, the guilty lay silent when they are exposed.

"You were the only one that could have saved her from those degenerate bastards. You chose not to use your heart, well guess what old man? Mine doesn't work either now. You could have shown her mercy, now I will show you none."

As he looked up I stuck my claw into his neck and

broke his trachea. I was covered head to toe in blood, my attire was drenched as though I had been swimming.

I looked around at the carnage I had wrought in a single night. I wondered if this was enough, *had I brought justice to the insufferable pain my mother had been subjected to*? The answer I came up with was no, one more villain needed to be extinguished and that was Sereigravo, the instigator of all my torment that had made me a vampire. The only way my soul could find respite was by eliminating the source.

I made my way back to the mansion. The night wore on, the crack of thunder resonated in the night sky. A violent wind from the north blew down the branches of enfeebled trees. Woodland creatures ran for cover into burrows and self-made shelters. Such an ominous night as a storm brewed in the land and inside my mind. Standing outside the keep I felt his piercing gaze upon me but I was not going to stop until this was over, or until I was dust. I kicked down the main door and looked inside to find darkness.

I wearily entered the premises, I walked into the main lounge to find the giant portrait of that woman Sereigravo looked at resting by the fireplace. As I approached to inspect it closer, "Beautiful isn't she? I always knew she would get away from me but I still wanted her."

I turned to face my mentor and arch nemesis.

"Sereigravo, you tricked me, how dare you try to make me lose the last shred of humanity I had left!"

"My dear boy, you were dead before you were even born."

More cryptic nonsense being excreted from his vile mouth.

"Do you know who that portrait is of, Crimson? Such an insatiable nymph she was in life."

"You know why I am here Sereigravo. Let's finish this."

Sereigravo began to pace the room and started to chuckle happily to himself.

"My dear, you really have no idea what is going on around you. It's no wonder she fled from me, perhaps she knew how you would turn out."

I was completely bewildered by what he was saying.

"Allow me to dispel your confusion my child, look at the portrait. You don't recognise her do you, how could you? You were not even born before this portrait was made."

I stood motionless, I could feel anger building inside me.

"Are the pieces still not fitting in place yet?"

The room felt like it was beginning to close in on me before Sereigravo said the next few words.

"Look at the portrait Crimson, it is your mother!"

My heart erupted in my chest.

"Everyday in the workhouse you were reminded of how she had skewer shaped holes in her neck, do you still not realise how?"

Sereigravo indicated at his elongated canines.

"Let me say in plain understanding, I loved your mother more than you could ever imagine. But as soon as she realised she was having you she ran from me. I pleaded with her to join me but she wanted to have you more than me. My desire for her led me to force the dark gift upon her, I was, however, unable to complete the deed as the mob arrived. I was about to avenge her death myself but seeing you in that workhouse, with all that fury pent up inside, I felt you could do your mother justice so I bided my time."

What was he trying to achieve in telling me this, my sympathy?

"In a time of great sorrow I gave you a proposal and you accepted. You have given your mother's soul respite by executing the men who killed her."

"They killed her because of you!" I screamed at the top of my lungs, my rage erupted into a barrage of swipes and lunges as I went to attack Sereigravo. He was far too fast for me, he evaded every attack with very little effort. As I began to slow down he jumped over me and as I turned around he hit me with the back of his claw. The force sent me crashing into the portrait.

"Well that was eventful wasn't it, are you pleased with yourself?"

"Why couldn't you leave us alone?"

I staggered to my feet having had the wind knocked out of me.

"I had more right over her than you simpleton, she was mine before she was ever yours."

"Why would someone as lovely as that like a mange-ridden dog like you?"

"Watch your tone Crimson, you know not of what you speak."

"I wonder could she or even any woman love someone like you?"

My provocation was working well, too well.

"Who would ever take an interest in a rancid flurry of faecal matter that has the resemblance of what a dog leaves behind?"

My final words were my undoing, Sereigravo seized hold of me and smashed me into every pillar, banister and piece of furniture in the building. He was so enraged that he would toss me into the air and jump above me to punch me down into the marble floor. After suffering a savage bludgeoning by his hands he threw me out from one of the stained glass windows in the lounge. It was a steep fall, and as I stopped tumbling down a hill under the window I came to an embankment of a swamp.

I had broken legs and my shoulder bone was protruding out of my skin. I had dislocated my arm and had several lacerations on my chest, face and legs. I was totally immobilised. At that moment Sereigravo landed near me. He looked over the swamp and began to smile.

"Whether you believe me or not it is irrelevant, but this is not what I had wanted for you, for us even."

If my jaw wasn't broken I would have continued shouting profanities at him.

"Alas this is how it ends for you, my dear boy, it's been a pleasure. Sunlight may not kill you as you are a vampire lord now but there are things in this swamp that will. Goodbye, sweet prince."

He took hold of my broken leg and threw me into the swamp.

WHERE THE BEASTS ROAM

Spinning slowly on the surface of the stagnant water, I began to think of what had led me to this point. My eviscerated cadaver lay bloated in amongst the decay of the swamp. Sereigravo's words echoed in my head: *'Dead before you were even born.'*

It finally began to make sense to me, everything had now been lost to me. I was so close to putting an end to my heartache but fate as always was against me. As I was being delivered into this world, Sereigravo was breathing his dark gift into my mother. The evil spread into her veins and then into me, but before she could fully turn the murdering vagabonds hung her. Residual darkness was present in me throughout my childhood making me impervious to the majority of harm.

Because of the greed of a single man I was damned, now I was left powerless. Before another coherent thought could materialise in my mind I felt ripples in the water's surface. I was feeling a sense of fear at that point because I thought something was coming. A damned man is he who kills the innocent, a damned soul is that which accepts evil into itself, and truly this day I was to be damned further.

A monstrous beast with armoured scales began to swim towards me. In the corner of my eyes I could see its snout and serpentine eyes. Its face was equivalent to that of my body, I could remember thinking *it could swallow me whole*. It had begun, the beast opened its mouth to reveal a yellow underlined roof with a legion of interlaced teeth. Both jaws had an innumerable number of razor sharp needles on the edges, mounted on tough scales. Its jaws snapped on my abdomen, I was tossed back and forth within the water as this demon-like creature attempted to sever some part of me. Had it not been for my broken jaw I am sure my shrieks of pain would have deafened anything with ears in a ten mile radius. My purgatory wore on, this absolute horror adopted a different strategy as every part of me was intact even though it was out of use.

It took a hold of my dislocated arm and the armoured hulk began spinning rapidly on its side. Despite the condition of my arm, my skin too was armour plated so not only did this atrocious beast spin but I began to as well, this however was the beast's own undoing. Being as formidable as it was, the beast knew nothing of my anatomy. My claw got lodged inside the roof of its mouth, it tried to shake free by tossing me back and forth but to no avail. The malevolence lizard actually made things worse for itself as the more it struggled the deeper my claw dug in.

Its blood began to flow rapidly and as it seeped into the swamp some nourished me ever so slightly. Its blood I had never tasted before as every other being I had devoured had warm blood. The creature became weak and as it lost the strength to devour me, I found the strength to put the beast out of its misery. It had no soft spot anywhere I looked apart from its enormous oak-yellow tongue. Like the rat in my mouth during my madness, I bit down hard on its tongue. Unlike me the creature did nothing, it had died from blood loss.

I hauled my mutilated carcass back onto the land along with the dead body of the gigantic beast. The blood I had absorbed allowed for my legs to heal but my shoulder bone was still protruding from my skin; that coupled with the new laceration I had from this watery giant meant I still needed more blood to heal fully. I sat down beside the body and as I began to slowly cut off the scales to reveal the soft, meaty underside I heard a noise. It was a deep, low sounding growl coming from the distance, hidden in the bushes.

I was truly intimidated, my jaw was working now so I tried to keep my angst as quiet as possible. The growl continued and I could hear the rustle of leaves. Whatever it was, it had a huge presence, the footsteps were heavy and the breathing was deep. It was a huge animal too, just like the dead fiend I was sat next to the only difference being it was a land dweller. I could smell the decay coming from its mouth in the air as this other beast began to stealthily pace in the near vicinity.

If I could survive an extreme wickedness in the water then I could survive this other voracious hunter.

I composed myself to confront this other creature that was slightly hidden in the brush but had its eyes locked on me. I saw its hide and mustered the courage to attack it head on. I rushed towards it armed with one claw and my jaws, my foolhardy nature was revealed to be ill advised. The new beast's roar was far more ferocious than mine and with a mere swipe of its hairy claw I was sent reeling back and fell on the dead creature from the swamp. I was dazed after being struck so hard, the forest was spinning around me.

My nausea calmed down and I arched my head forward to look upon my new assailant. A devilish creature as intimidating, if not more, than the scaled giant with the cold blood. Hair on every contour of its bulging frame, this beast had a round face and a slight snout. Its four legs were huge to support its awesome body. I lay witness to the extent of this animal's magnitude. It stood on its hind legs to reach a staggering height and it growled loudly into the night sky. The creatures of the forest dared not come out, it sniffed the air and returned to all fours once more.

Once again its gaze was upon me and it slowly made its way towards me. I was beyond fear at this point as I thought *either this animal dies tonight or I do. If this beast wins it gets no nourishment, however, if I win then the creature's precious life blood is mine.*

Once it was near enough I took a swipe at it with my working claw, I scratched its nose. This thoroughly infuriated the huge monster and it grabbed me by the throat in its mighty jaws.

Had it not been for my durable skin the beast

surely would have embedded those razor sharp canines deep within my neck. It threw me effortlessly into a tree, before I could compose myself it pinned me face down on the ground and began to maul my back. My shrieks echoed in the forest, the beast flipped me over and as I rolled I took another swipe at its face. This time I caused slightly more damage as blood trickled out from the side of its head.

This beast was not best pleased by my antics and I was slammed and thrown between trees, branches and bushes. The creature's onslaught on me was relentless and severe, I was hauled and mauled throughout the entire forest, slightly reminiscent of the beating I had received from Sereigravo. This sinister goliath had broken my jaw, the pain was extraordinary. It would take one well placed swipe from this hairy beast to decapitate me. Just as I thought it was the end for me again this new creature made the exact same mistake as the other and took a bite of my razor sharp claw.

As it writhed in agony I took the chance to strike it with my good claw, blinding him in one eye, but this colossal brute was still far too strong. I was swiped at once more with such a force that I was sent flying onto one of the lower branches in one of the trees. I looked to see the animal still in pain with its blood-drenched face.

As the hairy ogre composed itself I realised that I didn't really stand a chance against it. Relentlessly I was pursued by it, the tree I was on began to shake as it started to climb. I could smell its breath, it must have killed many creatures as it actually smelled like a slaughterhouse for cattle. Once it was in reaching distance it opened its mouth to take a bite off my foot, as soon as it did I raised my leg and, with the little amount of strength I had left, stomped on its face. It was enough to relinquish the creature's grip on the tree and it fell flat on its back.

If I did nothing now then I surely would have perished. The ravenous demon began to right itself but had its chest and stomach facing me. I leapt off the tree branch and landed right on it, I sunk my fangs deep into its hair, past the skin and into its precious blood. The animal roared in pain and did its utmost to shake me free. However once I started to leach off of it I began to regain health. The beast scratched, bit and fell on top of me but I wasn't budging, every moment that went by it got weaker as I got stronger.

It was the end for the beast, due to the blood loss the creature grew weary and fainted on top of me. The blood was so rich and full of energy, I understood why it was so strong and unyielding. The potency of the blood was equal to what I normally got from twenty mortals. Even though the woodland monster's heart had stopped I carried on draining the supreme blood and grew very strong. My shoulder bone had corrected itself and the wound it left had healed. The lacerations had disappeared and my jaw had realigned but more than that, I felt amazing.

When I could no longer taste sustenance coming from the blood I stopped and had enough strength to move the giant off me with one arm. I felt revitalised in a way that I felt like the beast itself. I put the new carcass on the other one I had inadvertently killed and came to realise something whilst looking at the two roaming beasts.

Not everything that gives you pain in life is designed to be the end of you, rather a new beginning. These two beasts had the potential to be the end of me, one more so than the other. Pain is but merely an avenue of travel we take in order to become stronger. It is not necessarily the case that what doesn't kill you makes you stronger, but surely makes you wiser. I looked at the two simple-minded killers and realised that they too wanted to escape the pain of life so they wanted to feed. Pain is weakness leaving you and wisdom alongside endurance enriching you.

As strong as I felt I knew I was still no match for Sereigravo. He would track me down by scent and finish me off once and for all. The only place he could not track me was in the murky depths of the swamp that led out into an open stream. I decided to head out but before I did I looked over at the two dead animals and thanked them for their sacrifice. Had it not been for them I would not have received the new lease of existence I now had. I gave them both the honour they deserved; the scaly one I returned back to the depths of the swamp and the hairy one I buried deep in the ground under some bushes. Even the sacrifice of a mortal enemy must be respected; with a tearful farewell to these freaks of nature I took to the swamp and swam out towards the open stream.

CONVICTION

I must have swum for miles, the depths and distance I covered could not be achieved by mere mortals. Once I was thoroughly satisfied that I could not be followed I resurfaced and made for the shore. I reached into my waterproof, leather-laced pocket to fish out my memoirs. All I found was soggy papers that were falling apart and dripping with ink. All my personal thoughts and history wiped out. I found writing utensils with material and began frantically rewriting what I had lost, lest I forgot. The world must know what I had been through. As I sat on the rocks and began inscribing I heard a slight cry in the distance. I ignored it until I heard it again so I went to investigate, I followed the wailing. I came to the shallows of the ocean and saw a woman howling off towards the open sea.

She was sat down but her feet were firmly flat on the rocks. She was wearing semi see-through clothing, like an assortment of scarves. She had long, luscious white hair that wafted in the air as a light breeze blew. She was gorgeous, the prettiest woman I had ever seen. Such a serene and attractive beauty, her gaze fell upon me and then I was able to fully appreciate her. She stared intently at me with those dark hypnotic eyes of hers. She began to lick her lips to reveal her big rigid teeth. She opened her mouth and I thought she was about to speak, instead she wailed heavily at me leaning forward towards me with her low cut dress. I will admit I was quite infatuated at the sight of her but the incessant wailing was highly displeasing.

The wailing continued and my patience grew thin, "Will you shut up woman, you could wake the dead with that sound!"

She stopped and looked at me quite upset as if I had done something wrong.

"Excuse me Miss, I didn't mean to be rude, I just thought the shouting was irrelevant." I tried to explain but she just looked on.

"Allow me to introduce myself, I am Lord Crimson. I am not from around here and just came to see what the shouting was all about."

She was being very despondent.

"Well it seems as though you are unharmed so I shall be on my way."

"Vampire!"

Her voice was not human, not even a mad woman's voice, it was as though there was an echo coming from her vocal chords. I walked back towards her and stood under the rock she was perched on.

"Indeed I am Miss, it seems we share a common

trait in that neither of us belongs to the natural world. So what then might you be?"

She took a deep breath as though she was about to shriek at me. She stared straight into my eyes and with her echoing voice replied, "I am a bean sidhe!"

I was slightly confused as I had never heard of such a being.

"Please forgive my ignorance but I have never heard of such a thing."

She began to smile, "I am known by the world of men as a banshee!"

I had heard of these so-called 'banshee' spirits in folklore but did not actually think they existed.

"Intriguing, I had always thought you were a myth."

She sharply angled her face to the side and looked towards the sky through the corner of her eyes before saying, "I thought vampires were a bedtime story."

She exhibited peculiar behaviour yet it was a pleasurable sight to see.

"Well, it seems as though we are acquainted now as to what we are but I don't know your name, if you have one that is?"

"My name is Fagnor, mistress of death."

"So tell me Fagnor, where are you from exactly?"

She raised her hands as visual aids and began to explain, "Where the land is surrounded by water opposite the larger land surrounded by water."

"So you are from an island that is opposite a larger island?"

She just looked on.

"What is the name of this island?"

"It is my island!"

"I see, so please enlighten me as to what a banshee is or rather does."

She got on all fours and peered down at me from her high rock.

"A banshee gives forewarning of a death in a family, we seek out those souls hounded by death and shriek so as to guide the angel of death to them."

I began to wonder about who she was warning of an impending death.

"Have you sensed someone to seek out yet?"

"Yes…you Crimson vampire lord!"

She began to cackle and I was bemused.

"What nonsense do you speak of?"

"Your sister is about to meet her doom!"

I felt a sharp pain in my chest, as though it was hardening, though the feeling was fleeting.

"What in hell are you speaking about?"

"Your sister Elizabeth, she is not meant for much longer in this world."

"How dare you speak of her? How do you even know about my sister?"

"It is my nature to know such things, my dear Crimson, I am attached to the mortal coil. It is what I was made for, to inform of death."

I ran up the rock to seize hold of this menacing spirit but as I did I received the back of her hand as she struck me down. I looked up, recovering from the blow.

"It is no use attacking me, I have no hand in her

destiny. All I know is what I have told you."

"You believe yourself to be of nature yet you do not belong to the natural world, how does that make sense?"

My words removed the grin from her elegant face.

"You forewarn people of impending death yet there is no real need for you as people die whether you warn them or not."

I could see this was beginning to anger her.

"So really what I am trying to say is, what is the point of you even existing?"

She shrieked and jumped from her rock onto me and a fight ensued. She was faster than me but not very strong, I was slapped and scratched by her but nothing substantially damaging. The fight wore on and we both began to tire. I took the chance to finally land a blow, as I did I hit thin air as she disappeared. I felt a tap on my shoulder so I turned around, as I did she scratched me.

I leapt forward to seize hold of her but she disappeared again this time reappearing perched on her rock once more, with her armpits resting on her knees as she cackled happily away. She wasn't able to teleport but she was too fast for my vampire eyes to keep track of her.

"Well your cowardice knows no limits."

"It is not cowardice but intelligence I have, really you have the brain capacity of an amoeba."

"You still have not answered my question bean sidhe, what need is there for you?"

She looked at me carefully.

"I belong to the mortal coil."

"That still does not answer the question does it?"

I could see in her face that she was losing confidence in her own argument. I leapt towards her, this time not to seize her but to further my verbal onslaught. I looked straight at her but she diverted her gaze.

"All living things have a purpose in life, people live their lives and die. Animals live their lives and die. Flies feed off dung and other rubbish to live but they still have a purpose. There is a use for everything in the living world but what is the use for you?"

She was silent and would not make eye contact.

"You see nobody really knows what a banshee does apart from wail in an endeavour to inform of impending death but is that really needed, are you needed?"

She snapped her head towards me and shouted, "What need is there for you blood sucker, you are a parasitic leech on mankind, you are not needed!"

I began to laugh as she looked at me, infuriated.

"Spoken like a philosopher, yes indeed there is no need for me in the natural world. The world will not be burdened by me but who said I care? My dear Fagnor, I care not about the mortal world, I don't look for reasoning in my existence. The world does not actually need me…"

The banshee looked on triumphantly. I continued, "…however it will suffer me, I am an affliction on mankind. Mortal men and women will fear me until the end of time. I do not rely on reason to exist, I make my own understanding, but you require them, they do not require you."

I had broken her, I could see the sorrow in her eyes. There was no need to strike her because I had already won the battle just by speaking. My conviction in my existence was enough to defeat her and her notion. The spirit did not cry or moan, she simply fell silent and lowered her head away from me. I began feeling the tightening pain from before only this time in my limbs, I began to walk away in case she had done something to me.

After a few yards she called out to me, "Wait vampire lord Crimson, tell me what then, what should I do?"

"How would I know? I have the brain capacity of an amoeba."

She shrieked at me then began to wail loudly into the air. I walked away, victorious.

When we have to explain ourselves to others in an attempt to validate our lives we need to have a very good excuse. We look for answers in others but really the answers lie within, we are not in need of acceptance from other bodies. If we can accept ourselves then others will have no choice but to accept us as well. I left the poor banshee without purpose but with better understanding. Perhaps our paths would cross again but then again I actually didn't care, she didn't matter to me. With my memoirs back in full record I continued to explore the land away from the sea. I came to a ravine and the most painful surges I had ever felt began pulsing up and down my body. This did not make sense, I was not evaporating and I had fed and was at full health. I wondered if the banshee had cast a spell on me, I began to convulse with pain, my body became stiff, I had lost control over myself.

Then something mortifying happened, a layer of thick brown skin began to wrap itself around my legs. I looked under my legs to see if I was being eaten alive again, it was then when I saw something horrific. The skin cover was actually coming out of my legs, the armour plating had opened and I was being enveloped by my own body. I felt a rip in my lower back, more of this wretched skin had come out from me and I was being encased. I could no longer move and was fully devoured by this 'skin'. I felt claustrophobic in this natural cocoon my body had expelled; as I tried to understand what was going on, a resin-like substance began to seep into this self-made vampire tomb of mine. I was now fully submerged in this liquid and immobilised in this casing. I lost consciousness.

DEMON IN THE MOUNTAIN

Sereigravo was standing there in front of me with a huge grin, telling me something indistinct. His words were blurred and I felt highly intoxicated as if I were poisoned. He took a step to the side to reveal a beautiful woman, at closer glance it was my mother standing there, had he brought her back to life? Sereigravo seized hold of her from behind and began kissing her neck, she was in clear distress. I tried to stop what was going on but I was restrained by iron shackles; he began to laugh at me.

Sereigravo removed his bandana and bit my mother on the neck, she shrieked in pain. I broke the shackles in anger and darted towards Sereigravo, but stopped abruptly as I felt something pierce my chest. I looked down to see a dagger's blade embedded in me, I looked at the hand holding the handle. I followed the arm to the chest then to the face, to my amazement it was Elizabeth. She said,

"You left me!" she screamed.

As she wrenched the dagger out, my face began to turn into ash and as I hit the floor I screamed in horror and woke up.

I was taking deep breaths in an attempt to recover from that dreadful nightmare. I looked around and I was still in that horrid skin layer. Light was seeping in and the resin had disappeared. I tapped the shell and it was brittle, I hit it heavy with a punch and dirt came pouring in. I crawled out from the earth like a ghoul and surveyed my surroundings. I felt quite lost as I don't remember being in this place before; what was the ravine was now a blossoming meadow. I was dumbfounded, I looked around and saw lush vegetation and mountainous areas with many trees. I began to wonder as to what could have happened but then made a shocking discovery. My claws had changed, they had become longer, much more like the talons on an eagle and were silver now. They almost looked like the claws on Sereigravo; I felt as though someone had cast an evil spell on me. As I touched my two claws together sparks began to shoot off, *were they really that sharp*? I had to find out. I took flight towards the trees.

Taking flight was quite an exhausting activity but now I found it very enjoyable and uplifting. I felt stronger and faster, now with these formidably enhanced claws I wanted to see what I could do. I touched the bark lightly with the tips of my claws and it began to fall off. I grabbed the bark with both hands and it broke away from the tree like picking up sand at the beach. But I wanted to do more; I ran swiftly towards another tree and took a swipe at it, then darted in the opposite direction. I turned around to look at the tree, I could hear creaking. As I did the tree began to tilt and fell over to one side. I was amazed at my fighting prowess, maybe the cocoon had something to do with my new disposition.

I walked over to see the extent of the damage I had done to the tree; I had swiped it clean leaving the stump fully visible. If the rings on a stump are any indication of age then this tree would be over a hundred years old. *Preposterous,* I thought at the time, *I don't remember seeing trees here before I was concealed in that skin but then I was in pain, I might not have seen them.* I dismissed it and began to explore the new terrain. I came to a very lush hillside with many grazing sheep. The sun was out and the herder came running over when he saw me, suspecting I was a poacher.

"Hey, hey I've already given you the agreed amount, why have you come back for more?!"

"I have no idea of what you speak, mortal fool."

"Hold on, I never made that agreement with you. Well, tell your brothers these sheep are my livelihood. If you think I'll give them up without a fight then you are surely mistaken. I have higher allegiance than you; dare hunt these and I'll inform the demon in the mountain and he will have his fun with you."

"I still don't know what your rambling is about, however if you do not put that primitive weapon down, I shall make you two become acquainted quite intimately."

He immediately dropped the pitchfork.

"Now clearly you have vampire issues seeing as how you assumed I am part of a brood that is hassling you."

The herder nodded.

"I am not after your sheep, nor do I care about you, however you said something about a demon?"

The man again nodded

"A demon other than a vampire?"

He continued to nod.

"Please explain all you know of this demon."

"Well he recently came to these shores but has been in this world for over a century. He came to live in the mountain because it makes him feel like he's back home. We came to an agreement: he gets to consume a sheep every six months and in return his presence revitalises the land and makes the sheep grow fat."

"He eats the sheep whole every six months?"

"No sir, he eats the souls. This demon is a soul devourer, all he asks for is one soul. He even keeps the vampires at bay and is quite effective in doing so, he says he hates vampires."

"Why does he hate vampires?"

"Well… because you are competing predators. Everything you kill means fewer souls for him."

"I see, well I think it's time I met with this soul-devouring demon."

"NO, no, I can't show you where he is, we agreed."

"Hmm…. maybe I wasn't being clear. Show me where he is or die!"

The man did not require further persuasion as he quickly took me up the mountain to a giant sinkhole.

"He lives down in there," the man said, pointing into the darkness.

"What does he look like?"

"Whatever he wants to look like, sometimes he looks like a giant sheep, grazing with all the others. I've seen him as a huge white bat hanging upside down in that hole. Once I've even seen him as a huge spider but in all honesty I have no idea what his true form is."

I shouted down the hole to get his attention.

"That won't work you know, he only wakes during the night. Somehow his vision is better that way. Incidentally, how are you able to stay alive in the sun? What kind of a vampire are you?"

"The kind that has long since lost the need to fear the sun. You say he likes sheep's souls?"

The man nodded.

"Well I think I should get his attention."

I took a hold of one of the sheep, the herder was protesting but it fell on deaf ears. He got in the way so I decided to kick him which sent him tumbling down the mountainside. I never saw him again. I stood over the hole and disembowelled the sheep; as its entrails fell I threw its carcass down for good measure. I was not afraid of any consequence as I had an enhanced body I wanted to try out. I waited for a while but nothing happened, it seemed I had to wait for night. So I waited in the sun, boredom took hold and I became tired. I must have fallen asleep after an hour, I was awakened by unearthly cries in the middle of the night.

I stood over the sinkhole to see if this demon was

there but nothing, this was a waste of time. I had other pressing issues to look to so I decided to head off. The moment I did I felt a strange tightening on my entire body. It wasn't painful like last time however, it was just restricting movement. As I struggled I shot up into the air and was drawn down into the hole with great force. I was accustomed to life in the dark, you can't see colours but with enhanced vampire eyes you can still make out outlines and shapes. I was in the sinkhole and it looked as though it had been there for a very long while. Stalactites decorated a tunnel within the sinkhole as stalagmites were protruding from the ground. It looked as though someone had been excavating for some time now as there was a careful organisation of bones and rocks. I heard many different footsteps approaching but could not see the outline of anyone.

"Why kill the animal if you had no use for it?"

The carcass of the sheep I killed was hurled at my feet.

"I had a use for the animal, it was to get your attention."

"You are indeed a brave soul, however this night you will meet your untimely demise, vampire!"

It was at that point I actually saw the owner of the voice. He was a hideous looking beast with seven legs of all different lengths and shapes. He had two arms: One looked like a giant human arm and the other split into two and resembled something like the branches on a tree. He towered over me and showed off his bulging muscles in intimidation. The demon charged at me, I rolled quickly underneath him and sliced one of his legs off. The demon groaned in agony and lost balance. He span around to punch me with his giant arm but I leapt out of the way before running up one of his legs, across his sternum and leaping over his head to slash him down his back. These were amazing claws, my speed and agility were too much for this mountain demon. However, my complacency was my own undoing, I became a little overconfident as I was getting the better of the exchanges. I misjudged a jump and the demon caught me with his enormous arm and impaled me on a stalagmite. He walked off triumphantly.

As I began to cough and splutter blood from my mouth, the demon stopped and turned around. My innards trickled down the stalagmite and began to evaporate.

"What kind of a vampire are you? That blow should have turned you into dust."

I was in no condition to even try and explain. Out of some inconceivable charity the demon hoisted me off the stalagmite and threw me to the floor. The hole the impaling had left was getting bigger as I was beginning to dissipate into the night sky. Then something wondrous happened, the demon's eyes began to glow bright green as he looked up towards the hole's entrance. His branch-like arm began to wave as though it was inviting something. My vision became blurry as I was fading but off in the distance I could see a sheep being slowly lowered down into the hole. The demon broke the animal in two over me. The guts and blood poured over me and I started to feel life again. I assimilated its bodily fluids and organs as my own and the mortal wound I was inflicted with rapidly began to heal.

"Demon, why would you help me?"

"There is such a thing as honour, even in enmity. Any normal vampire would have turned to ash immediately but you still survived. I know you, from your blood we are in fact allies."

I was completely baffled by this demon's claims that he knew me from my blood.

"Explain your cryptic rant, did you have a share in my mother's demise?"

"I do not know your mother or father for that instance. I am KrullKahn a true demon of the ether, another plane of existence sent to this world to rendezvous with a vampire. Something went wrong however, the ritual was not done properly. Our aura manifestation changed, I was summoned here instead and the vampire disappeared. I have been here for over a century and cannot return until my mission is over."

I was intrigued, maybe this demon knew about Sereigravo, if so then many pieces to the puzzle were coming together but there was only one way to find out.

"KrullKahn, are you from the order of Heaven?"

"I do not know of what you speak vampire, all I know is what the vampire was called who I was supposed to meet."

"So tell me the vampire's name."

"I believe he was called Alledantoro."

Revelation hit me like a tidal wave; this allegiance with the old madman, demons from another plane of existence and vampires goes back for centuries, what happened all those years ago?

"What is your mission KrullKahn? Perhaps I can help you with it. It would be in exchange for the favour you bestowed me with."

"My mission was to give this vampire a gift, but because of the treachery I was bound here and I cannot go back until the gift has been imparted."

"What treachery do you speak of?"

"The vampire must have altered the blood sacrifice upon the black and white floor. For more power I would imagine. My dilemma is to give the traitor his power or kill him and remain here for the rest of my life."

"What madness is this, demon? Blood sacrifice rituals, vampire powers and treachery."

"It doesn't matter now, vampire."

KrullKahn began to say something out loud to himself:

"This is the need to find the way, to find the means to kindly stay, to stay away from what we hold dear, to be away from what we loathe and fear, this be what the need is, this is the deed."

A cryptic sentiment, so random but I could relate to his pain. I joined in:

"I stare at the moon as I howl out of tune,
The darkness is menacing the mind
I fear that I am running out of time.
My time will be up and I will pass soon."

KrullKahn looked over to me and he came and sat in front of me before saying:

"The cloud sighs in complete derangement,
A little confided agreement,
A superior sense of endearment,
Like the grass during bereavement."

I replied in kind to his deep felt words:

"Reply to the last sigh, notice it didn't come from the sky,

The mud on your toes is wet, the trick is not to fall just yet,

Crying in a little corner we just weep like animals in the night,

We wonder what the reason is to fight."

KrullKahn continued:

"The glass isn't half full at all. We must all adhere to nature's call.

The freedom is yours if you can hold your own.

Be the savage, you are the dog looking for the bone.

You need it more than it needs you. Look for the secret, find the clue."

KrullKahn looked straight into my eyes, "There is more to you than meets the eye, vampire."

I assumed that was a compliment. Time passed in the silence of this demon's home and I remembered something he stated earlier.

"KrullKahn, you said before you knew me from my blood, how?"

"Your blood carries the signature of your forefathers, it is almost an exact match to Alledantoro."

"Absurd! What makes you think I am from the

bloodline of a ghoul whose brood attempted to destroy me, mind, body and soul?"

"You speak of such things as if I have knowledge of them, I am a true demon of the ether. My eyes see what once was and what now is, you are as transparent to me as day and rest assured my blood-sucking fiend, you are of Alledantoro."

It still didn't make sense to me, *if I am from Alledantoro then why would Sereigravo have anything to do with my mother? And what more do I make of them having a relationship as Sereigravo claimed*. I had no idea what was going on around me, but this conspiracy with my family and this order of Heaven runs deep.

"Vampire, is your offer to help still open?"

"What would you like me to do?"

"I will kill two birds with one stone, I will have my revenge and be able to leave this world. All you have to do is accept my gift of power that was meant for Alledantoro."

I decided to accept his offer, anything that would give me an edge over my adversary. As I stood ceremoniously in the sinkhole in front of KrullKahn, he began chanting.

"How do you know I will even be able to accept this power?"

"Your blood is all that matters. It'll work, I assure you."

KrullKahn's eyes began to glow green again, a bright light emanated from his body that illuminated the sinkhole. Every crevice was visible to me now, I began to feel my body vibrate. There was a blinding light; all I remember was waking up in the hole, it was morning and KrullKahn had disappeared. I wondered what power I was bestowed with.

I decided in order to progress I had to retrace my steps. I took flight towards my former retreat; the entire distance I travelled was different from what I remembered before. I found the swamp where I fought the two ruthless beasts, at least this area was the same. I scaled the wall up to the window I was thrown out from and jumped into the main lobby. The entire place looked as though it had been ransacked. A squatter saw me and fled, I wanted to talk to him and really wanted him to stop. I raised my claws towards him and I was about to pursue him until I saw he had stopped himself. Not of his own accord though, he was glowing bright green like the demon's eyes. It now made sense, the power that had been bestowed on me was telekinesis, I had willed the squatter to stop and my augmented mental prowess stopped him.

"Why are you here? Where is Sereigravo, the one who owns this mansion?"

"I've lived here for years, this mansion doesn't belong to anyone."

"Nonsense, do not lie to me or I shall rip your heart out from your throat."

"I swear to you, this mansion has remained derelict for a century. Looters came and now people who have no home sleep here in winter nights."

So it was true, I had lost a hundred years. I was in that cocoon for a century slowly transforming, all the evidence pointed towards it. The meadow, the tree, the demon and now this man telling me. I could no longer deny it. I released the man, who fled in distress. The remaining squatters I used as sustenance, the portrait of my mother was nowhere to be found and I had nothing to go on. Night drew on and I sat on the roof of the abandoned building without a hope. I started to howl at the moon:

"I saw the moon cry, shrivelled like a prune
Death dwells in the mind dunes
Knowing I will pass soon
All I can do is howl out of tune."

Then I smelt something on the air, a scent that I could remember from a long time ago. I decided to follow it lest I wander this earth aimlessly forever. I took flight in search of the origins of this odour and hopefully one step closer to my enemy, Sereigravo.

BLOOD TRAILS

I came to a distant shore many miles from the abandoned crypt. I came by following the same odour I had smelt many miles away. It was as though I could smell Sereigravo next to me, I was close to ending this enmity. But first I had to find him, I followed the scent trail. As I came to a mountain pass the scent trail had turned into a blood trail, the yellow stones stained with fresh blood. The grass was heavily saturated in decomposition, it looked as though it was a vampire feeding ground.

The bodies and bones of fallen people and cattle, whoever was responsible for this had no sense of decency, even amidst my madness I did not desecrate the corpses of those who I had fed off. This vampire had no shame or honour, clearly he had to be Sereigravo. I was getting near. As the smell of rotting flesh intensified, I heard the sound of fighting off in the distance and quickly made haste to see the origins of the noise. I came to a clearing on the mountain and began to observe a spectacle whilst being partially hidden behind some rocks.

A vampire I had never seen before was battling a small contingent of knights. He was clumsy and careless, had a total lack of style and finesse. He reminded me of Emmanuelle as he fought but had no honour. He tore off two limbs from one of the knights and spat at him as the knight screamed in agony on the floor. Then with the severed body parts he sought to beat the remaining knights to death, clearly lacking in any moral fibre. He stood on top of one of the fallen knights and looked on as reinforcements came. He disembowelled the first few and bled dry the last of them; the sight was a sickening display of savagery.

He began to laugh at the destruction he had created, standing triumphant in the middle of the dead bodies. I started to clap as I revealed myself to him, he spun round and focused his eyes on me.

"Bravo my dear vampire, that was an amazing master class of brutality."

"Who might you be, admiring fiend from the shadows?"

"I am Crimson, a vampire from a far away land."

"And why would you come here from afar?"

"I am searching for someone I know, as I came I happened upon your savage demonstration."

He began to laugh smugly to himself.

"Who were they?" I asked.

"Human scum, warriors from a local kingdom that have been hunting me and my Master for years. They have become more resilient over the years because our appetites have grown. However they will never be able to take us down."

"I don't believe I caught your name."

"Oh, please forgive my impetuous attitude, I lost myself after I killed all these mortals, I am Lord Raikarnor, bringer of death and I formally welcome you to our shores."

He welcomed me to ruined, blood-splattered surroundings with no signs of life or providence. This vampire and his Master had brought waste to this place and had sucked it dry. Even though I did not show it I was feeling a deep hatred towards him already.

"Thank you for your hospitality, so tell me, Raikarnor, of your history here."

"Well like any other, I started off as a human. I was suffering from a terminal illness and had become very weak. No doctor, physician or witch could bring me from the precipice of damnation, that was until he came. My Master breathed new life into my eroding bones. I felt the power of a hundred years of absent minded evil… and suffice to say I liked it."

I could not help but ponder on how he romanticised death and destruction. He had such a morbid outlook on his reality it would surely catch up with him one day.

"Tell me Raikarnor, how did your Master save you from damnation? Surely by making you into a vampire he has sealed your fate."

"You look like a vampire of high esteem, if not of

pure regal standing. I will politely ask you to refrain from unkind words projected at my Master."

I nodded in acceptance and he continued.

"No I was actually saved from damnation, I didn't have a hope in the world. What would you know of a dying man's pain? I was at my wits end and in an incredible display of mercy my Master delivered me from the hands of the angel of death."

Clearly he was devout to his cause, but that devotion made him blind to the stark reality he was in.

"So then tell me of your story, Crimson."

"I, like you, was embittered by pain, you see as a child I was born an orphan. I never knew my father or found out what had happened to him. All I had to go on were the taunts I received whilst I was made to slave away in a workhouse; the owners of which had my mother hanged for absurd reasons. As soon as I decided I wanted no more of the torturous beating I received, I fled and a rich man found me. Taking pity on me from my state he adopted me. Growing up I had never felt at peace as I did with that man and his family to which I had been incorporated. Unfortunately that was not meant to last as my new-found family started dying, I was left with my adopted baby sister. One fateful night I met a vampire who gave me a choice. I chose to escape the nightmare that had become my life."

He was hooked on my every word.

"Please continue, I wish to know more of your origins and your life as a vampire."

"My Master told me of things I never knew existed, he already had an acolyte at his disposal but with my addition, our brood was becoming formidable beyond measure. As brothers we would carry out our Master's wishes and I fell in love with the evil within. Through the new found existence I encountered love, madness and betrayal."

He was astounded by my tale and his eyes were transfixed upon me as if I had some power over him.

"Tell me of this betrayal."

"I was sent on a mission to absolve a mistake I had made, it turned out the one to orchestrate my demise was also the one to give a reprieve from a life of humanity. After being torn from the mortal coil by the reason of my grief I sought revenge, however it was not to be. I confronted my fork-tongued Master only to be pummelled almost into nothingness and left to be devoured by the most atrocious beasts nature has ever spat forth. Of course that was not the end of me as I survived them. Soon thereafter I underwent the most terrifying metamorphosis that resulted in enhanced capabilities of this immortal body. After an encounter with an amazing demon with his own story, I wanted to retrace my steps to cover the ground I had lost. Then when I thought I had lost all chance of redemption I happened upon a familiar scent and that led me here."

My baffling tale had Raikarnor mesmerised, "I am astounded by your amazing history, did all those things really happen to you? I never heard of such turmoil. I think that you should join our clan, it's only the two of us; however we are a lot better than the other two you joined with, we won't betray you I assure you. What do you say Crimson? Would you like to join our brethren?"

"I have no desire to be part of another brood, I have issues to attend to."

Raikarnor was quick to persuade me otherwise, "But we can help in your endeavours, we will do our best for you and in return you could help us with the hunt. Just looking at you I can see that you far surpass my physical prowess, in fact your claws resemble my Master's. A demon of your talents should not be wasted. Join us and we will join you in your quest for revenge, what have you got to lose?"

He had a point, I had nothing to lose despite joining with uneducated killers. If what this meagre vampire said was true, that he was indeed being mentored by a Master vampire, then that vampire could help me kill Sereigravo.

"Very well Raikarnor, I accept. You have made an irresistible proposal."

His face lit up and he became erratic with joy, jumping off boulders and rocks. When he started to dance on the bodies of his victims I began to growl loudly which made him stop. It was not that I had any sort of affinity for the fallen but this vampire was even less, in my eyes, than Emmanuelle.

"I think we should go, please lead the way."

"Yes, yes right away let's depart for our mountain retreat. I can't wait for you to become a new addition."

Night was beginning to fall and my new found

allegiance was becoming ever more annoying as he waffled on about his and his Master's exploits. He told me how his Master killed orphans for fun and how they liked to desecrate gravestones of those that they drain. It seemed as though I might end up killing them myself, inadvertently doing the knights a favour, however I had to remain patient as they would probably be the only edge I had over Sereigravo. We walked for a mile or two and it occurred to me that I didn't know his Master's name, so I enquired, "Raikarnor, a thought occurs; you haven't even divulged your Master's name to me, is it a secret?"

Raikarnor smiled and replied, "He's an amazing tutor, taught me everything I know. He showed me my potential and how to reach it. Really the capabilities to what I can achieve are endless under the tutelage of Master Sereigravo."

I felt an eruption in my chest, this repugnant pile of grotesque existence was in the service of the very enemy I sought. I stopped dead in my tracks as I was walking with him.

Raikarnor noticed as he walked besides me, "Are you malnourished Crimson? You look unwell."

I could not even conjure the words as the feeling of unadulterated hatred was so overwhelming, so I merely nodded at him to avoid any suspicion of my intentions. He continued to walk on and I was conflicted as to what I needed to do at that point in time. *Do I wait until my quarry is in sight? Or do I interrogate him now to tell me Sereigravo's whereabouts so that I only have one of them to fight*? My hand acted of its own volition. I struck him with my claws on the back of his head, the blow sent him hurdling into a boulder. He regained his composure and was enraged by my behaviour.

"What are you doing, you imbecile?"

"You talk more than you think, Raikarnor. So trusting of other vampires but then why would you not trust? Considering one helped save you from death. It may be insightful for you to know that I am actually hunting your Master, how lucky am I to have caught your revolting scent on the wind so that you could tell me where I can find him."

I could see desperation on his face as he realised that I was on a quest to kill his Master.

"You will never get to my Master, you will be dust before this night is through!"

With that he began hoisting boulders onto his shoulders and lobbing them towards me. My physical prowess had peaked to such a point that with mere claw swipes I was able to effortlessly shatter them into rubble. He continued his onslaught which was becoming quite infuriating. As he hurled another boulder at me I suspended it mid-air with my telekinesis but I had become angry with him after learning everything about him. The fury I felt must have manifested itself into my power and the boulder disintegrated into dust. I was learning much about this amazing gift given to me by KrullKahn, that was actually meant for Alledantoro.

I could use it offensively as well as defensively. As he went to pick another boulder from the heaped pile besides the mountain base, I concentrated on his right claw; the effect was a small explosion on his wrist. I had blown his hand clean off with the power of my mind. I walked up to him as he lay on the floor in agony, cradling his injured limb.

"I have no quarrel with you, Raikarnor, despite that fact you have no grace whatsoever. All I wish to know is the location of Sereigravo."

"I will never tell!"

I concentrated on his knee cap which resulted in him losing another limb, he gave out a sharp cry.

"I will continue on in this fashion until you have nothing left or until you tell me what I need to know."

He began to laugh through the pain.

"You think you have everything under control but you don't even know the half of what you are into, Crimson. If what you say about your mother is true then all I have to say is the pig deserved it."

I immediately took a hold of his head and held it in between my claws.

"Brave vampire you are to say such things, loyal minion you are to keep secrets but foolish cattle you are too. If you are here then he won't be far off."

Before he could utter another word I compressed his skull within my claws with such a force that his head collapsed and he ruptured into ash.

I cleaned myself off from the vampire's remains and continued in the direction we were originally headed. He may have only been a fledgling lord with massive potential but I found him wholly annoying. I could have dealt with the situation better in hindsight but sometimes even spur of the moment decisions can lead to good things despite being negative. Sereigravo was close as I could smell his foulness in the air, I was getting closer to the end of my heartache. I trekked on.

THE PACT

Raikarnor was a brave warrior who had the will to carry out his Master's wishes to the death. His absent-minded perspective to attain his Master's approval reminded me of when I was in his place. He served Sereigravo who, even after a century's interlude, was still my sworn enemy. I vowed to myself at that point that until I had wiped Sereigravo off the face of this earth I would not rest nor move on. A viper's bite means that you will either die from the poison or the bite; on the off chance you survive you will forever fear that animal till the day you die. A vampire's bite means either you die or end up killing others; I am a cancerous mass on the bloodstream of humanity and once my affairs were in order I no longer wished to be here, the sight of Liza was enough to make me realise that there is no place for monsters in this world. Evil has no place here and now, or for future generations to deal with. I was now on my final mission.

As I sat down to write about the encounter with

Raikarnor, I felt as though someone was watching me carefully with the intent of harm. I had nothing to fear as I could smell their scent on the wind. Knights were strategically arranging themselves around me under false belief of stealth. One fool-hardy knight with cruel intentions swung his weapon at me out of nowhere. I dove out of the way, but my memoirs got sliced in two and his huge axe was entrenched in the ground where I was sat. The knight removed his frightening weapon and I took a very detailed look at this new brave soul. His armour looked frivolous as it was decorated with diamonds, emblazed upon a gold plated fixture. His greaves and gauntlet had fearsome ridges that looked razor sharp. The knight had a helmet I had never seen before, more ridges were mounted on the headpiece but instead of edges it had diamonds mounted on the ridges, with an emerald the size of a man's fist fixed upon the forehead area. His axe matched his outfit but was still deadly, even though it looked like a decoration piece you would find in a wealthy person's home. I began to chuckle to myself at this sight.

I was, however, completely taken by surprise by what happened next, the knight attacked me with his axe. His movement was swift and fluid in motion and power. I moved out of the way of his various attacks but they were all mere inches away from actually touching me. This warrior was far more tenacious than any knight I had ever encountered, even more so than any of the vampires I had met on my travels. He was not to be taken lightly so I decided to concentrate on neutralising this awesome foe. I utilised my superior speed to disarm him, as he swung with his axe I zipped behind him. Just when I thought I had him, he showed me his versatility, with the sharpened hilt of his axe he stabbed me in the lower abdomen. As he wrenched it out of me he leapt into the air and kicked me in the face with a spinning kick as I tried to pursue him.

Unfortunately for this talented brave mortal, he was up against me. As he went for his killing blow I suspended his movement with my telekinesis. He began to groan as his movement had become restricted for reasons he could not understand. I lifted him into the air and took my time to dust myself off and collect my memoirs before dealing with him. I lowered him to eye level whilst he was still struggling in the same position of suspended animation.

"Who are you and what do you want?"

He tried to break free from his invisible bonds.

"What trickery is this, vampire, have you no honour? Put me down and let's finish this the way it is meant to be!"

I wanted to take a closer look at his axe because I wasn't able to fully appreciate it during the violent exchange. I willed it to my claws with my mind to the amazement of the mortal. On closer inspection it was made from durable stainless iron and had been sharpened to an extent of insanity. *Why would mortals carry such weapons that have the capacity to be their own downfall*? As I touched the metal with my claws pieces of it began falling off, I was amazed at my own physical prowess with no arrogance.

"Release me fiend, you have no calling to this world. Let me end your suffering!"

I was most amused so I humoured his delusions of grandeur. I released him from my hold and he looked at his axe in my possession, I believe he might have felt incomplete without it. I gently threw it over to him, no sooner than I did he leapt into the air, took hold of his axe and slammed it into my chest. As it stuck in my chest the knight backed away, his blow had barely penetrated my reinforced hide.

My transformation had made me an almost impregnable walking fortress. He stood there looking at me astonished as I yanked the axe calmly out of my chest. With a simple slice of my claws I broke his primary weapon in two. With a gesture of my hands and the power of my mind I tore off his helmet and brought him to his knees. For theatrical purposes I asked him a cliché.

"Any last words, pathetic mortal, before I dismember your body?"

He said nothing. As I advanced to deal the death blow I stopped, his face made me stop. I had seen his face before, I looked upon him and began to feel as though I knew him somehow. I could smell his perspiration and I shook the feeling off. I went to deal the blow again and I saw his eyes. They were green and sparkled majestically in the pale moonlight. The harder I tried to kill him the more my body froze, I felt as though he was using magic on me.

"Come on devil, finish it. This charade is becoming tiresome."

I had an indescribable feeling of longing towards him for reasons beyond my understanding. I released him from my hold as he looked at me with complete confusion.

"Have you lost your mind vampire, where I am from we kill mortal enemies."

I looked away from him trying to understand why my hand stopped of its own accord.

"Look at me vampire, I want to you to look into my eyes as I turn you to dust."

So I turned to see what he had in store for me this time. He ran towards me brandishing a decorated dagger. No sooner that he began to run he too stopped in his track, we were standing in front of each other and the earth fell silent. This wasn't magic or nature, this was lunacy.

"What's the matter brave knight? Why have you stopped? You kill mortal enemies don't you? Here I stand, kill me, release me as it were."

My words did not reach his ears, he began to look at me in the exact same way I was looking at him when he was at my mercy.

"Who are you vampire? What magic are you using against me now?"

"Please, don't flatter yourself, you are of no consequence."

"If that were so then why did you stop yourself?"

I had no reply, I began to walk away.

"Wait, where do you go vampire?"

I was too confused and made haste away from this madness. The knight ran after me and stood in my path.

"Step aside mortal, I have no time to play games with you."

He stayed in my way in defiance.

"Do as I say or I will decapitate you where you stand!"

He didn't flinch, I went to hit him with my claws but the same cursed feeling of familiarity hit me again and my hand wouldn't touch him.

"What sorcery are you using against me, noble knight!?"

"How dare you say such evil words against me? I am Lord Lazarioss, General of the armies of the north, rightful heir to the throne and a true believer. I do not rely on witchcraft I believe in the one true God, who is sufficient for me."

"Well Lazarioss I have matters to attend to, I care not for your belief so if you please remove your wretchedness away from me."

"Not until you tell me who you are, I have seen you somewhere before."

"Really? Well that is only possible if you are over a hundred years old. I am a very old, insidious presence, human, you do not know me from anywhere."

"Even if that is the case then we still share a commonality."

"What makes you say that? We have nothing in common."

"Then explain to me why, on two separate occasions, you were not able to finish me? Explain to me why I feel as though I have seen you before?"

I hated this feeling, this creature continued to test my patience.

"You have no answer for me do you?"

I was frustrated because he was right, he began behaving as though he was with a friend.

"Tell me who you are, noble fiend?"

"I am Crimson, a vampire from a far off land. I am here in search of another vampire. We have a history that I wish to end with his remains."

"A vampire hunting another vampire, you are the ultimate antithesis in the realm of evil."

His jest was pathetic.

"This may sound strange to you, vampire but I feel as though I have known you all my life, and by all means please make a mockery of that."

Under any normal circumstance I would have done but the feeling was mutual, as though I was looking at a little brother of mine. I felt as though I was in the company of a long lost friend. I felt my cheek muscles contracting, I helplessly began to smile at him and I did not know why. He began to light a fire.

"Please sit down for a while."

I sat down looking at him over the blazing fire, his features almost looked like my own when I was human.

"So tell me my smiling fiend, this vampire you seek. Why are you after him?"

"It's a long history, knight, one I do not wish to divulge."

"So be it, can I at least help you in your endeavour? Seeing as how you are doing my kingdom a favour."

"As talented a fighter as you are, you are of no use to me."

"Now who's flattering themselves? I would have had you had it not been for your magic tricks."

"You say this as if it meant something to me. On the battlefield you do what is required to win, death is indiscriminate of anyone. You have your deadly moves and I have what is in my arsenal, deal with it human, you lost."

Instead of a sharp reply he began to smile and nodded his head at me in agreement.

"I did not come here looking for you Crimson, I came here because there is a dangerous duo of vampires that have decimated this half of my kingdom for years. I knew of one of the two's last known whereabouts, I encountered you by accident. Enough was enough so I came here with my army to destroy them despite the heavy casualties we would have won, God willing."

"Well it might please you to know that one of them is already dust and the other will be soon."

His face lit up, "I shall assist you in the final hunt."

"No you will not, as I told you before you may be gifted in the art of war but this quarry is mine alone. I need to be aware of my surroundings in the last fight. You will just get in the way."

"Your arrogance is profound vampire, how were you aware of your surroundings if you barely escaped my first attack?"

"This may bruise your ego to know but I allowed you to get as close as you did. I could sense your presence as well as your army that is looking at us right now."

"Really, tell me then, my faux omniscient friend, where is my army?"

His nonchalant ignorance was insulting my intelligence,

"Allow me to educate you then, your army that is hidden in many different places around us. The forty archers near that small hill, the thirty foot soldiers hidden near the rocks to the north, the twelve scouts that are constantly running in a linear trek and your second in command that is a hundred yards behind you lying down in that bush." I said, as I pointed out the various locations. His smile grew ever bigger and he could not help but laugh as he was impressed.

"You are truly remarkable, well at least tell me how I could be of assistance to you? You are doing my kingdom a service. There must be something we can do for you."

"There is, you know these lands better than I, tell me where I can find the keep of the vampires that have terrorised your kingdom?"

"So be it, Dante!"

The man lying in the bush came running over to us.

"Yes, my lord."

"Tell this vampire of the mountain keep of the fiends."

The knight turned to me, "Follow that northern trail until you come to a divergent path. Follow the left trail which will lead you to the forest retreat on top of the mountains."

"Thank you, noble knights, it's been a pleasure."

I darted away and that insufferable human followed.

"Halt!"

"What is it now human?"

"You are so melancholic I find it humorous, but I wish to make a pact with you."

"There are no such pacts with men and the damned."

"Under normal circumstance that is true but you are different. My heart tells me that you are someone valuable to my kingdom. That could be understood merely by your mental disposition for killing vampires. In my gut I know you from somewhere, I will make a pact with you regardless because I believe it is the honour you deserve from a fellow warrior. I will be of service to you before my life is out, on my family's honour I will serve you somehow for sparing me. I owe you a debt that I will repay, God willing."

He had his hand out waiting to be shaken. I firmly shook his hand and we both smiled at each other in gratitude before I took flight to the mountain pass.

END OF THE HEARTACHE

I trekked high up into the mountain path following Dante's direction, I came to the divergent path and began contemplating my journey. The path I travelled was much like this trail, forking off in two different directions, each decision made resulted in irrevocable consequences that I was constantly beset by. It was appropriate that I came this way as this trail was complimentary of my entire existence, the choices we make seal our fates. If I went one way I would never know what lay beyond the path of the other trail. *What would have happened if I had said no to Sereigravo when given the choice? What would have happened if I had never run from the workhouse? What would have happened if those beasts didn't attack me or if I hadn't met KrullKahn*? So many thoughts dispersing all around my cerebral cortex, sundering my mind leaving me with fearful censure, I may have done some things I shouldn't have. I proceeded despite a weary heart.

I came to the forest on top of the mountains amidst the cloud and the dense air. I had no necessity for oxygen but could fully feel the pressure at this altitude.

"Alas, my wayward son returns to me."

I turned to see it was my arch nemesis, Sereigravo, abseiling down the side of a large tree using his claws. His feet landed on the ground softly and as he made his way casually over to me, the bark on the side of the tree fell away completely. Sereigravo walked straight up to me.

"Welcome to my humble abode, Crimson, demonic assassin of redemption."

"It has been a long time, Sereigravo."

"Sereigravo? I see you have broken away from being a vampire lord."

"What do you mean?"

"My dear boy, you encountered the shell I believe?"

"Yes."

"I have been a Master longer than you, I am fully aware of the transformation process. The liquid that entered the shell was secreted by your vampire skeleton to make your skin as hard as diamond."

"We have business to conclude Sereigravo, I did not come here to exchange pleasantries and reminisce the days of yore."

"Yes, yes of course but all in good time, First, tell me what you think of our new home?"

His blatant ignorance was embarrassing but even among enemies there is a level of honour that should be adhered.

"It is pleasant, spacious, well ventilated and serene, however it is not as comfortable or welcoming as your previous lodgings."

"Indeed I agree, I am planning to make improvements."

He began walking away from me and towards the summit. I followed him and found him sat on the edge of a cliff face, looking over a small waterfall next to a pristine valley. I sat on the edge as well, adjacent to him with my back facing him. The water fell down into a gulley that led towards the lush greenery-covered wilderness. I lay witness to the magnificence of unaffected beauty that I had never seen as I had mainly lived my entire existence in the cities and towns.

"Look out there Crimson, see the power of nature. Behold its wondrous beauty that is not constrained by any means. It has been here on its own accord and if it remains untouched it will continue to flourish."

He propounded as though he was about to sing, I had other thoughts.

"I have seen things of majestic beauty that I never knew could exist. I am in awe of the natural and metaphysical exponents that exist and shape our environment. I do not understand the awesome magnitude of life but I have begun to respect it, even love it, in some degree. Ironic how I hated it whilst I was alive."

"So you share my vision that things of beauty have a duty of care to be loved by us?"

This charade was amusing at best.

"Sereigravo, I agree with myself, I will never concur with the instigator of my doom."

"I see even after a century you still harbour feelings of hostility directed at me."

"Maybe after the savage bludgeoning I received off you or perhaps after being left at the whim of animals of daunting proportions with appetites to match. Yes, maybe at that point I had true hatred for you considering it was your machinations that had my mother killed and put me on the path of self-destruction. However, I have had time to reflect on my situation and during my travels I have met characters completely divergent of who I am and what I stood for. I realised things have a purpose and there are understandings such as honour and respect even between enemies."

Sereigravo intently listened while sat right next to me.

"My dear boy, you are truly a sight to be reckoned with."

"Since then I have come to realise my place in the world; and that is that I have no place in the world. My family is dead, the last remaining member I did have must be gone too as it's been over a hundred years since I saw her. You see, my dear mentor, we are parasitic entities that hide our shame in a shroud of self righteousness when really there is no need to do such things. In life we are a filthy scourge that has been beset upon mankind and we are both masters of that scourge. I will not rest until we are both dust, however I will make sure I follow your lead in that respect."

These weren't the words he wanted to hear.

"You make some superbly colourful commentaries, I will not pretend that you have come back to join my side. However before we conclude our affairs, I wish to know with sincerity how you have been over the years and tell me of some discoveries."

Best to grant a dying being's last request, "Well I think it would be best if you started."

Sereigravo happily approved.

"Well where to begin? Since I left you I suppose. I had no more need for the mansion, a vampire in a house by himself is but a corpse in an extravagant tomb. I left every single one of my expensive possessions and took flight towards the north. I found a pristine wilderness and decided to make it my new home, fresh surroundings for a fresh start. There is a neighbouring kingdom that is expanding, at the time I thought it was the best resource of food but in this seclusion I was not happy."

Sereigravo always was the storyteller but I wasn't going to interrupt.

"I required a subordinate to try and regain what I had lost, I found a dying man surrounded by loved ones who were praying for him. I gave him a choice and without any hesitation he accepted. I was very fond of him from the beginning, he reminded me of you and Emmanuelle but because of his illness, despite the dark gift, he could never become a Master. So for many decades we did as we pleased in this kingdom. Constantly I had nightmares of you, sometimes they were so bad I thought you were still around. In my lunacy I would go around and decimate orphanages in an attempt to be rid of you."

It seemed I had more of an effect on him than he did on me.

"My senses would return and I remembered how I left you to the whim of fate. I had my acolyte, Raikarnor and things have been good for me. That is until now, the clouds darken, I feel the grip of reality tightening and realise it is about to end. Before I give you the tactile pleasure of telling me Raikarnor's fate, I already know. I can smell his blood on your claws."

His plight was as pathetic as his argument.

"You are upset about your loss but you forget I am your creation, the way I am is the way you made me to be through your actions, deceit and cowardice," I said.

"Thank you so very much."

"You are scorned, I know this, but the guilty is he who instigates."

It was my turn to share as Sereigravo listened,

"Since the swamp I fled in fear through the open seas lest I fall prey to you again. I met a banshee and had a colourful verbal exchange with her, soon thereafter the shell took a hold of me. I woke to find a world transformed and my physical magnificence amplified, I was feeling invincible. A short clash with a demon from another dimension showed me no matter how strong you think you are, there will always be someone stronger than you. We began to talk about our histories in brief and I came to know of his mission."

"Mission, what mission?"

"Well it may please you to know that his mission was to serve Alledantoro."

Sereigravo's eyes lit up and he took a hold of my shoulder. I peered over to him scornfully and he released his hold.

"What did he say about my Sire? Tell me Crimson."

"He said nothing of Alledantoro except that he hates your Sire and wanted revenge, but he could not get it by himself, so I helped him."

"How did you help an enemy of Sire Alledantoro?"

"It was easy, I merely accepted the gift that was meant for Alledantoro, his mission was complete and I became more formidable than ever."

"What gift did he give you, Crimson?"

"The one I am going to use to kill you with, Sereigravo. I caught the scent of that rotter in your service, followed it and here we are at last."

Sereigravo scoffed nervously, "I see, well all good things must come to an end as the philosophy goes, but perhaps not today. I ask you now Crimson, that if it be possible to put our past behind us, to do so. Instead of an ending why not make this a prelude, what do you say, my dear boy?" Sereigravo asked, putting his hand on my shoulder once more.

"We are wretched things, Sereigravo, we have no longing to this world. There is no element that tethers us to this reality, it is as you said before. We have a duty of care to the living world but how can we achieve that duty by being here and representing the destruction of the living world. I do not want this out of some previous personal vendetta, rather it is my duty."

I removed his claw from my shoulder.

"We have business to conclude Sereigravo, come."

I waited for him back in the heart of the forest where we were reacquainted. He was not sad, scared nor had he any other emotion visible on his face. With a calm demeanour he stood opposite me a few yards away.

Sereigravo immediately darted towards me brandishing his claws, I adopted a similar tactic and we engaged in the middle of the forest. Our claws ripped through clothes, bones and blood, we hacked away at any part that we could. Pieces of blood and skin began to fly up into the air, we were at a stalemate in blood-soaked fury so both of us jumped back. We looked at each other, growling heavily and watched each other's wounds heal. Sereigravo flew over to a tree and hacked it down in one swipe, as it began to fall in my direction I leapt out of the way. I turned around and had lost sight of my target.

I wearily began surveying the woodland ground to see where he might be, constantly looking over my shoulder to make sure he wasn't behind me. I heard the sound of an object flying quickly through the air, I looked up and a large chunk taken from a tree came and hit me. The large projectile was of trivial consequence but it wasn't meant to hurt, rather it was the beginnings of an onslaught. Sereigravo was running across the tree tops and every now and again hacked off the top of trees and lobbed them down at me. I ran from the bombardment, his accuracy and speed were frightening but I was able to evade the remainder of his ammunition. No sooner had Sereigravo stopped throwing giant tree pieces at me that I encountered another tiresome problem; something took hold of my leg as I was running and hoisted me up onto a tree, I looked to see what it was whilst being suspended several feet off the ground. A rope had lassoed itself to my ankle and a boulder was acting as a counterweight on the other side of the tree. Sereigravo had laid traps, I cut myself free from the feeble ensnarement.

I landed on my feet, as soon as I stood up Sereigravo was in my face. He had stabbed his claw deep into my chest, his claws were the only thing sharp enough to penetrate my reinforced body. I could feel my power dwindling and darkness overshadowing the world around me. Sereigravo was about to kill me but something happened, something I didn't count on. I saw a ghostly figure walking about in the distance, it leapt from tree to tree and disappeared into the canopy and then a blood-curdling scream tore through the forest floor. It was so loud that Sereigravo tried to cover his ears, as disorientated as I was I pulled his claw out of my chest and pushed him away. The scream stopped and, as he came towards me again, I kicked him on the chin with such a force that his feet lifted off the ground and he fell on his back. By the time Sereigravo had composed himself I had taken flight and was hiding in the rich foliage near the tree tops. I needed a little time for my wound to heal.

"Come out Crimson, what were you saying about cowardice before?"

I got the feeling that I was being watched, not by Sereigravo but by another entity. I heard rustling nearby, as I looked in the direction of the noise I felt a light tap on my right shoulder, I turned quickly to see who it was. No one was there, I turned the other way and to my absolute shock, right next to me was the Fagnor. She looked deep into my eyes and I looked at her, not knowing what she was doing here. Before I could say a word she took hold of my collar and kissed me passionately for several seconds before pushing me off.

I didn't know what to make of all this as she looked as though she hadn't aged a bit, despite seeing her a century ago.

"Remember me, my darling Crimson?"

"What are you…?"

"Shh… be quiet he's listening. OK look, I'll distract him and when his gaze is on me you finish him off OK?"

"OK but…"

Again before I could finish she began jumping down the branches. She reached the forest floor and Sereigravo saw her. She began dancing, much to the resentment of Sereigravo. I saw the opportunity, from the dizzying heights of the forest top I leapt down towards Sereigravo, Fagnor looked up which in turn made Sereigravo look up as well. As he did I came crashing down to the forest floor and slashed his face with all the power I could muster. That, coupled with the gravitational force, made for a devastating blow. Sereigravo staggered back, I got up to confront him now that I was fully healed. The damage was frightening, the liquid from his eyes began oozing down into the claw marks I had made in his face.

I began spinning around with my arms out, acting as an infernal tempest I started perforating his chest and stomach. Once my whirlwind of fury was over I looked upon him. I could see the inside of his chest cavity, as though I had hollowed him out like a pumpkin, Sereigravo still on his feet began regurgitating blood. I became more determined at this sight and with a backhand hacked down a tree that landed on him. I used my telekinesis to hoist the tree in the air slightly above Sereigravo and I proceeded to bash him with it several times. Sereigravo incapacitated and fatally wounded, lay helpless under the tree at my mercy. Fagnor jumped on the fallen tree and peered down playfully to look upon Sereigravo. I looked into his eyes and despite the injuries he began to smile. I stabbed him as hard as I could with my claws into the remains of his chest and finally brought my hundred year old heartache to an end. As Sereigravo erupted into dust, Fagnor jumped off the tree, all the pain and angst within me climaxed, I roared as hard as I could into the forest. My insurmountable fury made me strike the fallen tree, rendering it into two. Fagnor looked on confused at this spectacle and I fell to my knees.

I didn't know what to do with myself, the pain within me made me feel like crying. The triumph for me and my dead mother made me want to sigh in relief and everything I had lost coupled with everything I had gained up to this point left me confused. Fagnor came and sat in front of me, angling her face flirtatiously to one side.

"You truly have conviction, vampire Crimson."

"And what do you have, bean sidhe?"

"I have insight, I see that some things in life that were meant for evil can be used for good."

"There was no need for you to do that favour upon me, benign spirit."

"You left a hole in my heart the last time we met, now I feel as though it has healed. I did this for me not for you. I have purpose."

I smiled at her in gratitude.

"Fare thee well sweet prince, I shall see you on the other side."

She leapt onto my head and off into the forest; I never saw her again. I sat there wondering, *now that it is all over what should the next step be*? I had made my mind up that once my affairs were in order I would extinguish my own existence.

I looked towards the heavens and, with the hope that I had given my mother's soul some respite, I aimed my claw to my chest.

"My beloved mother, sweet Alisha, my darling Liza and respected elder Marioss. I have done justice today, may your souls be at peace. I come to join you."

As I went to impale myself with my own claw, an ominous wind began to blow.

LINEAGE

The wind became ferocious as it intensified in speed and breadth. The trees began to sway violently and I could see static electrical currents sparking up from the ground. The ash that was once Sereigravo began spiralling up in a vortex above the electrical currents and I started to fear the worst. Then sudden silence, the wind and electricity had disappeared, I had no idea what had happened but was glad it was over. That was until I began to feel the ground shake and the wind and electricity came back more violently than ever, suddenly a blinding light appeared a few feet in front of me accompanied by a strange glow and small lightning strikes in the near vicinity. I could hear thunderous rumblings coming from this light and then, unexpectedly, a bolt of lightning shot out and knocked me to the floor. The electricity disembowelled every tree in the near vicinity, I looked around at the carnage and wondered what could have done this.

I turned back, the light had disappeared and in its place a tall dark figure had manifested. The collosal figure, hooded in a black cloak, stood still on the darkened grass where the small lightning strikes had struck, the electricity was still fizzing around this individual. I saw this creature raise its arm to reveal, from the baggy sleeves, claws of epic proportions, like mine but they shined like rays of the sun as though they were actually made of diamond. As the creature with the fantastic claws revealed its face I saw to my privilege that it was in fact a vampire, one which I had never seen the likes of before. The face was pale as the clouds, it was cracked with scars but retained some signs of pristine power. His fangs were too long to be concealed by his mouth so they protruded past his lips, he was a sabre-toothed fiend. He towered high above me and was heavily built by muscle mass. I felt quite intimidated to say the least.

"Well done prodigal son, you have succeed in your conquest of redemption, I congratulate you."

His thunderous voice boomed, I was speechless and slightly scared to reply or enquire about anything.

"You clearly are worthy of being a demonic assassin of redemption."

I was still having difficulty in speaking so I just continued to watch him in a slight state of shock.

"It seems as though you are lost for words, allow me to dispel this ailment. I am Sire Alledantoro!"

My whole consciousness was rocked, I could not believe what I was laying witness to.

"How can this be? You went missing."

"Yes, I believe that is what it would have looked like. My poor boy Sereigravo was truly lost."

"What fevered dreams am I experiencing with my waking eyes?"

"I assure you, my dear boy, that this is no dream, while my appearance is hard for you to approve of, it is necessary considering what you have done."

"What I have done? What do you mean?"

"Killing your own kind in the name of supposed vengeance, you have no idea of the consequences you have wrought. Although you cannot see it due to your present manifestation it doesn't mean that you will not suffer a heavy burden."

"I am having difficulty understanding you."

"Then I will speak candidly; I am Sire Alledantoro an old and powerful vampire from a long line of vampire history. You are my descendant, the blood in me is the same in you."

My heart sunk, a wrenching pull of vertigo took over me as though my soul was imploding within me.

"I am sure by this revelation I have stunned you once more but make no mistake you are from my family, in life and in death. When I was a man I had a child, I had to leave my family to serve my brothers in the order. A long tradition in the order has been to turn into vampires. It was my turn; when he came of age I turned my son into a vampire too. Tell me Crimson, what do you know of your father?"

"I believe he died in a war."

"How feeble, and who informed you of this lie?"

"I was told that by the slave workers."

"A likely story but highly inaccurate, you see your mother and father were both passionately in love with one another, until your father was summoned by the order; he became a vampire and I became his mentor. I hope he taught you well, by the looks of things he has."

"What lies do you speak of, I have never met with my father."

"On the contrary my dear boy..." He knelt down and took a fistful of ash that was Sereigravo, "...You knew him very well."

He began sprinkling the ash down.

"You lie to me devil!"

"Is that so, why do you find it hard to believe? Because you killed your own father? Because you don't want to associate with what you were born to be? Your approval is obsolete as the facts remain. Sereigravo was my son and your father, once I ascended into Siredom he went mad with loneliness, in his hysteria he went to his estranged wife, your mother. She tried to run away but he caught up with her, due to his own cowardice he lost the love of his life but a spark of life was left; you were born into this world with your mother saturated in her own blood and sent to the gallows. I congratulate you on finishing what you set out to do."

I was distraught beyond compare, this wasn't possible.

"You congratulate me? I killed your son and you don't care."

"I watched you intently from another plane of existence, whilst I loved my son with all my heart I understood how unstable he was. I did not want any harm to come to your mother, after all, she too belonged to my family, I could not protect her from him. You are all I have left now my dear boy, you are all that matters now."

"You expect me to stand by your side, after all that has happened?"

"What else is left there for you but to join the order of Heaven?"

"The order of Heaven?! Just as the mad man said."

"Yes, I saw how you dealt with an ejected member of the order. You see once you join you do not leave or betray us. If you do then things become 'difficult' for the person in question."

"Did he try to leave your brotherhood?"

"No he didn't leave but he didn't do something we asked him to do, so we drove him to madness through poisoning him and killing his family. You however took him out of his misery."

"You are the epitome of evil, I spit on you and your brotherhood."

"The mouse telling the lion it's disgusted."

Like Sereigravo, Alledantoro was also a storytelling sycophant.

"The idea is not about being evil, it's about power, over the minds of the masses, having control over everything. Having absolute power is what we aim for and we will not stop until the world is in our grip. The time is almost here."

"So you think you are omnipotent now, with your brothers?"

"We have objectives to reach, all of which grant us power in the upper echelons of society but we work behind a veil unseen by the masses."

"Blasphemous malefactor, you dogs will rot in hell!"

"Is that so, after all this time what do you care of righteousness? Can you undo the carnage you caused or lives you took? No you can't, hypocrite, we are the same you and I. However you still have the right to join us, I cannot invite you but you can ask for initiation of your own accord. Thus taking your rightful place by my side."

I was incensed at his bravado and psychosis, "I will not join you, foul nuisance, and may God curse you and your brethren throughout the ages."

"Truly, well you will not be spared either. We may have blasphemed but you shunned God's grace when you accepted the darkness. Farewell damned soul, I return to the ether."

"Wait! You have been to the ether, how is that possible?"

"I see I have finally caught your attention, being that you are not an honorary member I cannot tell you."

He began to fade into the air.

"If not as an honorary member then tell me for being part of your lineage."

Alledantoro stopped fading and came back.

"That is much better, respect is much more pleasant to listen to than distain. I will not tell you of details but will tell you what happened to me. I was in the great hall surrounded by my brothers between the pillars. The time was accurate with the day of year, I recited our prayer upon the transport module and was taken to the other side via the black and white route. I was to meet a true demon of the ether named KrullKahn but another demon altered our arrangement. I fled from this demon in a world I was not accustomed to, as time wore on I started to adapt, my body was nought but a cloudy manifestation in a darkened realm. Now I am powerful enough to phase in and out of both worlds, also I am fully aware that you took the power off KrullKahn that was meant for me. I am not offended, consider it a gift, now I will go back and hunt this other demon. The question is, will you join me?"

Such untold history was whirling inside my infested brain, it was hard for me to understand and appreciate. This was beyond any fairytale history ever told.

"I am truly intrigued by all the things that have happened around me without my knowledge. I am the son of a vampire whom I have killed, the same vampire who took everything precious from me. Now I learn I am from an ancestry of ancient vampire progeny being given the chance to take my rightful place in an order whose quest for power will lead to world domination. An order that for millennia have corrupted and controlled the world with the aid of unfathomable creatures from another plane of existence, am I right so far?"

Alledantoro was not amused by my antics.

"You are a trivial pursuit Crimson, I do not know why anyone in my family bothered with you. I will not waste anymore time on you, rot here for I care not!"

"Please hear my proposal before you go. I wish to say something that will interest you."

"Speak and do so quickly, you are a concern not worth taking."

"Hear me as this involves you, I have learnt much in my new animation, things that would not be possible as a mortal. In that respect I am thankful, but knowing what I know I cannot stand idly by. When Sereigravo was still here I had a duty to fulfil, I made a promise to myself that once that duty was complete I would extinguish my own existence. The duty was to eradicate everything in my life that caused me harm as a human and as a vampire. I laid waste to my brood because I thought it best served the interest of humanity that Liza belonged to. Once I completed that task I was about to destroy myself, that was until you came. Now that you are here, I still have a duty to do."

Alledantoro squinted his eyes, not because of his vision but because I had confused him.

"Are you serious?"

I simply nodded my head with a smile on my face. Alledantoro walked straight up to me towering way above my head, he knelt down to look me straight in the eyes.

"Basically what you have just said is this. Now that you know that I still exist you will not leave this existence until I am no more, what's more is that you plan on destroying me yourself, is that correct?"

"In simple unequivocal terms, that is exactly what I said."

Alledantoro stood up to his full stature and laughed whole heartedly, his booming laughter permeated the remainder of the forest. He knelt down once more to look at me, "Is this a challenge, Crimson? Do you wish for a fight to the death? Surely you know you are no match for me despite your enhanced abilities."

"I owe a duty of care to the living world despite not being from it anymore. You are right, I have fallen from the grace of God in accepting darkness into my life but here is my penance."

"Interesting as you are either very brave or completely stupid. I could kill you at will, you will be dust before you could even think of a move to make against me."

"Then do so, respected elder."

I defied him, exposing my chest. He looked at me with critical observation and began to smile.

"You are of my blood and I will honour any challenge from a worthy opponent. Your physical prowess is lacking, when you are ready I will be waiting. Do what you have to do to become worthy for me and then, when you are ready to fight, call upon me in the northern kingdom and we will conclude this dispute. I fully accept your challenge Crimson, demonic assassin of redemption."

I leant forward slightly in respect for him, "Then we have an accord, with the utmost respect my dear elder, Sire Alledantoro."

He slowly backed away with a smile on his face,

he began to laugh and as he did he faded slowly back into the immaterial. I had one last mission to undertake, but for this foe I could not win on ability or strength alone. I needed assistance as I truly was no match for him. A thought came to mind, unwillingly an agreement was made to me a little while ago. I remembered the noble knight, Lazarioss the general of the armies of the north would be a formidable addition to my arsenal. If his offer was still redeemable I would have his army at my disposal. Alledantoro, no matter how fearsome, could not take on an army by himself. I had purpose, a destination and method to reach that destination, so I made haste for the northern kingdom and to my human ally Lord Lazarioss.

THE PATRIARCH

There sometimes comes a moment in life where you think you have done all that is needed. You rest your weary soul under a blanket of relief as you know that your affairs are in order. It is then when you realise that there is a disparity in your life that needs addressing which means your work is not done. I was so close to the end, in reaching my own relief when Sereigravo was gone but then his Sire, Alledantoro materialised and burdened me with further responsibility that I could not dismiss. These are the actions we take and we must abide by the consequence. Killing Sereigravo meant that I had to meet Alledantoro, now I would put an end to my savage past so that the future would be tranquil for mankind.

I made my way out of the thick forest, when I could see the mountain base I decided to take flight but to my dismay I did not have enough energy. I tried my best to stay in the air but nothing worked, my power depleted and I fell all the way down the mountain face. Finally I reached the divergent paths heavily disorientated and nauseas after the continuous rolling. I needed a moment to recollect feeling in my inert posture. As I came to full awareness I looked towards the other path that I did not take the first time round. It led up a hill that looked like it was covered in flowers, the sun was setting on the horizon and the illumination was a beautiful sight against the back drop of the serene pale blue sky. Then, to my wonder, a dark figure appeared on top of the hill and with hand gestures started beckoning me to advance to the top of the same hill. I was weary as it could have been Alledantoro but my curiosity peaked and I made my way up the hill regardless.

What I saw on the other side befuddled my mind completely: lush green grass growing tall and wavy, beautiful blue ponds containing all manner of marine life, poultry frolicking in rich foliage and healthy trees scattered generously throughout this area. It was a gorgeous oasis that I had stumbled upon, at first glance it looked the same as the one I spotted whilst I was talking to Sereigravo. The slight waterfall that disappeared down into the gulley confirmed it as I had in fact walked to the pristine wilderness that I observed from above. It made me realise the idea of causality, there is a cause for everything, and there was a cause for my new found mission. There was a cause for my vengeance against Sereigravo and being in the oasis, there was a cause for that too. Life and death are in synchronised harmony together and you cannot have one without the other. I began to ponder a little at this display and what it could mean for me.

Alledantoro informed me that I would be burdened by something, I walked up the divergent path different from the one which led me to Sereigravo and an unlikely audience with Alledantoro. I wondered what would have happened if instead of taking that path I had taken this one and came to see this vision of tranquillity. I walked through the area taking in the sights that enriched me with a sense of well being, as though this was my reward for vanquishing my foe. Though deep down I knew it would only be over once Alledantoro was destroyed. I headed to the northern kingdom though this time I took the scenic route through this little piece of visual bliss.

The day became night and the sky darkened to welcome the howling of the moon. I could not help but compare myself to this strange heavenly body. Just like the moon I am heavily scarred and without a friend, even though Lazarioss fitted the nature well. I felt alone without anyone to call my own. I continued to walk until I came to a vastly open area surrounded by mountainous surfaces. As I surveyed the area I saw the same darkened figure and felt overwhelmed again. Although this figure was a fair distance away I felt nervous and, it seemed, with good reason. It looked as though every time I blinked this figure had made a significant portion of the way towards me. After blinking no more than four times this dark figure cloaked in purple robes, hooded and with red silk underlining, had traversed the entire distance from being at the mountain top to standing a small distance in front of me.

For reasons unknown to me at the time I felt a compulsive urge to fall to my knees and lower my head, without thinking about it I did. The dark figure slowly walked over to me, with its hands concealed under its cloak. The creature began to talk to me, his voice barely discernable.

"Salutations… little… spawn… at last… meet."

"Greetings I am pleased to see you, you honour me with your presence."

I felt as though I could raise my head slightly but could not look him in the eyes. I don't know what brought me to speak like that but it was as though his presence demanded respect whether I was willing or not.

"I… been… watching… Crimson… what… result… of… this?"

"I am not doing this out of vengeance or spite rather I feel as though it is my duty to do so. My family harbours secrets of murder and villainy in the name of self righteousness. As a vampire I represent everything wrong with the world, I am trying to bring balance to the diabolical machination of certain individuals, vampires today are a plague."

"Do… know… me… son… I… patriarch… vampires… first… father… I… plague… kill… me?"

"Please excuse my insolent tongue if it offended you, I will tear it out if it has. Forgive me my Lord, my heart knew who you were but my mind did not. This is the single most greatest honour that I have been bestowed with in my entire existence, please accept my homage to you, Sire."

"not... displeased... Crimson... your... burden... heavy."

"My lord I am relieved to be in your graces, I have suffered innumerable hardships I am not afraid of anymore that I may be afflicted with. I do not say this in arrogance. I am merely accepting my fate no matter what it might be."

I wondered what he meant by a heavy burden.

"You... suffer... loss... kinship... redemption."

I was slightly confused, I thought he was being cryptic with me but then again it was hard to tell. What kinship is he talking about? As I had no living member of my human family left. I did not dwell in thought too long as it seemed I was to be questioned further.

"Why... killed... Raikarnor?"

"He had no honour Sire, he was a liability with no cause or intelligence. He would have met his end some way or other, I merely spared him from continued depravity."

"Sereigravo... honourable... killed... why?"

"That was vengeance my lord, that malefactor set in motion irreparable consequences on me due to his own weakness. At first I was motivated by hatred but then by duty to my human family. I am aware that it is quite paradoxical of a statement to make considering I have killed the innocent but truly that is how I felt at the time."

"Kill... father... shame... now... Alledantoro... why?"

"Alledantoro is the root, it all started with him so it will end with him, I owe it to myself to see it to the end."

His interrogation took a different turn.

"I... father... vampire... essence... power... kill... any... request... kill... Alledantoro?"

"My lord you certainly are powerful to possess such a powerful influence on us, I will respectfully decline your offer."

"You... fear... promise... self... kill?"

I began to smile at such a notion,

"No my lord I do not fear the end, it will come regardless of victory or defeat. I refuse such an offer because even in enmity there is such a thing as honour."

"My...son...my...pride...give...you...blessing...go...the ...east...watchful...aid...power...go...at... peace Crimson."

I was touched by his words to such an extent that I felt a slight tear run down the side of my face. I began to smile as I knew I had his full favour. With my posture still in submission he walked over to me and gently stroked my head and lifted my chin slightly. As he did I slowly gazed at him, his eyes looked regal in colour. They were glowing bright purple so that they illuminated part of his face hidden behind the hood, he was smiling at me. I could not have asked for more of a prestigious visit from an entity of this calibre. He walked off as he approached me, such an ancient presence yet completely unknown to the entirety of our race. The progenitor of the vampire, the father of our kind.

His last words still echoed in my mind, it couldn't have been Lazarioss as he was in the north. I thought the more allies I had then it would definitely tip the scales in my favour, I had nothing to lose so I adhered to the advice given. Instead of going to the north I detoured to this supposed aid.

THE ENEMY OF MY ENEMY

I was becoming very tired, the air was wet and heavily humid. To make things worse I hadn't fed for a while. I came to the eastern region as instructed and wondered where this aid was or even what it looked like, apparently I was being watched by it. I felt at that moment it was best to rest and reconvene with my journal, my story might not get completed so any record made was valuable. I sat near a tree in the dead of the night and began inscribing events that I hadn't commented on up until that point. As the night wore on the temperature began to drop and the air became dry which brought slight relief. As I came to the end of writing about my meeting with the first ever of my kind, I heard rustling in thick grass nearby a stream. It could have been the aid I was to meet but as I looked on it was actually a lion which came out.

The lion had a huge furry mane that decorated its face and followed all the way down its body to its groin. It made him look bigger than he actually was, I could understand why many creatures feared such a beast. I was not impressed, not because it couldn't cause me harm; rather I had seen other beasts that made this one pale in comparison. It roared loudly at me, I may have intruded on its territory but I wasn't going to leave either. I returned the favour and gave him an unearthly roar which definitely intimidated this alpha male. It licked its lips and wet nose before jogging away slightly. Unfortunately for him I was hungry and he was powerless against me. I took flight over to him and sliced the huge cat into three distinct pieces. Its blood was a nourishing beverage and as a snack I took out its enlarged liver and began chewing on it. The flavours that I induced from the tender meat gave me the indication that this animal fed well. I went back to the tree and closed my eyes whilst reclining on the base.

I don't know how long I was made to wait but it was irrelevant as there was no real time limit that I was constricted by. I started thinking strategy about the last fight that would take place, I didn't want to make the same mistake I made against KrullKahn and I surely doubted I would be given any favours by Alledantoro if he were to land a fatal blow. I had never faced a vampire Sire before so I wasn't going to allow myself to assume anything. I would need to be ruthless and fast in my attacks, I would use the knights to keep him at bay whilst I would regroup before continuing the onslaught. If everything was calculated and our attacks were synchronised to inflict the maximum amount of damage, whilst keeping him off balance, then there was no doubt that he would surely fall before us in little to no time. The only thing that worried me was what he may have in his arsenal. As fantastic a fighter as I had become, it stood to reason that he, being a Sire, would be that much better than me. I had to expect the unexpected and go on instinct during the encounter.

"Shh…Shh I see you
Can I be one or should I be two
I am quiet like a ladybird, with feathers
Like the soft, cool, calm winter weathers,
Oh look at him, he looks so sweet
Like a tangerine that wants to meet,
He must taste lovely, him surely I would love to eat
I would love to take a bite out of him much
Perhaps get a taste, a glance or a slight touch."

I stood up sharply to look around at where the voice came from, I saw no one and began to think I had imagined it.

"Is someone there? I was told to come here to meet with you."

No reply came which made me feel slightly stupid just talking to myself. I sat back down.

"Does the demon not see me with his own two eyes?
Does he not know that I too have spies?
Will he anticipate my special surprise?
Why does he still live whilst my kind dies?
Perhaps his thirst for death is insatiable to ignore
It leaves me to wonder what I was made for.
Is he going to sit under the tree until day?
Or is he willing to play and have something to say."

I was not in the mood for such surreal games as I had more pressing issues that better deserved my attention instead of this intangible noise that seemed infatuated by me.

"I do not know what game you are playing, whatever might be your intention for me I assure you I have no desire to consummate some type of relationship with you. I was informed that you were to help, if that is the case, do so instead of wasting my time."

"And he calls me out so that I react
We are both deadly fiends that is a fact,
Whilst it might trouble him to see
I revel in the heart of anarchy,
He must realise that I do not adhere to the mortal coil
To the victor go the war spoils
So if he wishes to be able to win the game
He too must speak the same."

"I grow tired of this idiocy, farewell troublesome error and my thanks to you for this useless pursuit."

I began to walk away highly frustrated as I could have mustered the army forces by now and confronted Alledantoro had I not been here. An echoing laughter emanated from the tree but I had lost my patience with the surreal nature of this area. I decided to depart, as I walked away a thought came to mind. I ran back to the tree to enquire about something.

"You there, are you still in the tree? I understand now what you meant."

There was no response and I began to feel as though I may have done something wrong once again by losing patience.

"I think I understand your cryptic message and wish to engage you now. Can you here me in there?"

Still no response. If I were to have the voice to reengage me in conversation then I had to act instead of enquire, so I swallowed my pride and said:

"I am a stranger from a far away land
I have travelled the water, rock, grass and sand.
I have a heavy heart due to personal torment
Every day and every second all I do is lament.
I am the personification of evil despite my intention
I have been tortured ever since my conception.
I do not know what hurdles lay ahead
For all I know, tomorrow I could disintegrate from being dead.
I embarked on a mission of redemption to kill my makers
God willing I will be able to disprove any naysayers.
I walk alone in this deadly world that wasn't meant for me
I am plagued by death, my existence has been a complete travesty
But I will make amends in some form or other
When I pass I will not be given a coffin, shroud or cover.
I will return to the dust in an explosion of ash
We vampires multiply like a rash
But I will destroy those in my bloodline
So I ask you now, will you be an aid of mine?"

There was no response and I felt I had shamed myself after that slight poetic confession. As I started to walk away the voice came back:

"So you finally realise the best way to talk, it's interesting how much better you think when you begin to walk."

"All I ask is that you present yourself to me and help me put an end to the world's misery."

"All in good time my disgusting little friend, first give me your ear to lend."

"Ask away unearthly entity, I eagerly anticipate the sight of thee."

"In order to fully engage me, I ask that you disembowel this tree."

I took a step back and began to ponder if that was all I had to do in the first place. I took a swipe at the tree base and stood back as it fell down. Then a sight of wonderment took place, on the trunk of the tree I saw that the wood was not still but was moving as the motion of waves in the sea. I touched the surface and it began to fizz loudly, like it violent reaction was caused by my claws. Then I saw who owned the voice; a huge muscular arm came out of the truncated tree, followed by another the same length and size.

The arms looked like the muscular one KrullKahn, had but this creature had two. Then the amazing demon revealed its head to me: devilish horns the size of my arms were standing out from his forehead. He stepped out with his cloven feet to stand in front of me. He was slightly taller than me but was bulging at the seams with vein popping muscles. His appearance was definitely demonic as his skin colour would alternately flash blue then red in regular intervals. His face was long and had a darker shade than the rest of his body and finally, to fit the bill, he had a long tail with fur at the tip.

He looked like a pitiful caricature of the devil and I

had no doubt he would be just as despicable as Satan. Truly I had never marvelled at such a being before.

"*Ta da* vampire, finally you understand how that game was played."

"Why didn't you just tell me to break the tree without singing? Or better yet, why didn't you just break free yourself given your strength?"

"That is not how demons work. We don't do whatever is asked of us, first you have to do something for us then we give you something."

"Interesting, well then tell me, what did I give you and what have I received in exchange?"

"You gave me slight entertainment and in return I gave you my corporeal presence."

"How excellent that must be for you, so you live in a tree?"

"Oh please I don't think so, I am from the ether."

"So you too are a true demon of the ether, perhaps you know KrullKahn?"

He began to laugh, "No I am not like that despicable cur, he is a true demon that feeds off the souls and life force of living beings."

"So what is the difference?"

"The difference being that I kill and eat whatever I desire, even other ether demons. This KrullKahn you speak of, a long time ago was about to be my next victim but some vampire swapped places with him. I hunted the new prey but somehow he got away. I believe you are familiar with him. He belongs to some ancient order obsessed with global power. I watch their activities, I watch what they do from the ether summoning more demons to their bidding."

The pieces were beginning to fit.

"Tell me your name, I don't think you have formally introduced yourself yet."

"My apologies, I am Gregorian of the ether and I am here to give you some invaluable help."

As soon as he said this a twitch developed in his hips and they began to sway rhythmically side to side, this neutralised the veneer of his intimidating sight and I began to snigger under my breath.

"Yes very funny it would be to you. I am not accustomed to the elemental configuration of this realm and this is what happens to me."

I was still laughing, "Please forgive me I had no idea."

"Yes please continue to mock me, for the record I had no idea how grotesque you really are. The ether can be deceptive but this plane shows you for what you really are."

I composed myself, "Very well, let's just leave it at that shall we?"

He nodded as the twitch moved its way to his shoulder.

"Gregorian, you are an enemy of my enemy, so we have a common ground. Just because we are, on some level, mortal enemies doesn't mean we can't come to some sort of agreement."

Gregorian was interested in this understanding.

"Yes I believe we can reach an accord that best serves both our interests. I want that vampire dead, what do you want?"

"I want the same, though I am not able to deal any significant attack upon him."

I had no reason to trust this obnoxious ghoul, his mannerism was as bad as his smell. In all honesty I was acting on blind faith, out of some innate responsibility to the old one I had just met. By the way he was standing with all those muscles bulging I failed to see how Alledantoro would even be a concern. Why did this demon need a lesser vampire like me? The truth came painfully quick. We had established some sort of common ground but his pose towards me looked as though he was about to devour a chunk of my head.

In the end what choice did I really have? Gregorian and I had an understanding now, and I didn't see the need to jeopardise it. I needed him so I questioned him on the best course of action.

"Good so now that we've got the terms out of the way let's proceed to strategy."

"Absolutely, time is of the essence. You are too fickle in this moment in time to have any real affect on him so not only will your body need to transform but so will your powers need to be enhanced further. To hurt him first you have to get to him, which means you will need to ascend into the ether."

"So what you are suggesting is that I need to become a vampire Sire in order to be effective against him."

"You will need to be what he is if you wish to complete your objectives, however there is a manner of incantation and ritual that needs to be invoked before transformation is possible."

This seemed a bit far-fetched for me but I decided to adhere, "Very well, tell me what I need to do."

"A vampire of your calibre must have a special room where rituals are practised. You must exercise the dark rites there."

"I have no such room at my disposal."

"Well then we are at an impasse, to the best of my knowledge every Master vampire builds one of these rooms in order to ascend."

"If every vampire has one of these rooms, then my former Master must have had such a room."

"It would stand to reason for him to have one, you must go to him and ask to use it."

That was a pity, seen as how I had ended his infernal existence.

"Such a thing will not be possible."

"Why is that?"

"Because he's ash now."

"I see and how did he meet his end?"

"I stabbed him in the chest after finding out he attacked my mother."

"That is quite strange, so why are you after this vampire that I want dead?"

"Let's just say it is complicated."

Gregorian looked at me with a blank stare as the twitch had moved down into his knee and made his leg manically bounce in one spot. After a moment of an uncomfortable silence, "Clearly you have personal issues," he remarked with a slight smirk on his face, "Moving on, you must find this room which is normally located in the catacombs of a vampire's retreat."

"In all the time I had lived there I did not happen upon such a room."

"That's because you had no knowledge of it and you didn't read the signs."

"What signs do you speak of?"

"To get to the sacred chamber follow the red lines, they are the veins of the room that give the retreat life. Follow them to the opening, the core."

"Once I find the entrance then what?"

"Well obviously you will need to open it, in that endeavour I cannot help you however once inside the ritual can begin. Stand on the transport module that is of two different shades between the two ceremonial pillars and recite the sacred prayer, but before you can enter the holy area you must spill the blood of the impure."

The most astonishing thing about this was the depth of knowledge this demon had about vampires. Whilst I was curious I had neither the time or patience to query.

"Surely you mean the blood of the pure, a virgin?"

"And since when have you obtained the knowledge about dark rituals?"

The twitch moved into his chest making it pop up at random intervals.

"I was informed by my Master that it was the blood of a virgin that he needed to ascend."

"Well clearly he was lying or he had another agenda in mind, which is irrelevant. To invoke such powerful evil you require tainted blood, so hear my words and cast your doubt aside. Once you are on the module and reciting the scared prayer, you must do so in a proportionate fashion."

"Please elaborate."

"You can only say the prayer six times in six breathes on the sixth hour in order to be successful."

"What is the prayer?"

After I asked he tossed over a small scroll to me, I unfolded it to find an inscription written in unfamiliar characters:

عند محاذاة الشياطين اسمح للشيطان ان يكون لي

"OK demon, I cannot read this and I believe all this is becoming somewhat of a joke."

"I have watched you for a while and in the short space of time I have known you I can say that you are a fool. Whenever help comes to you, there is always an outburst from you because you quibble at its price. That's why everyone you have ever loved has died due to your impatience and now you are not willing to take heed to my advice. So be it, impudent dog, I shall be on my way."

He started walking away with the twitch in his shoulder again. What he said was true, my impatient and abrupt nature drove away that beautiful woman, Liza, even that lovable banshee. I was not about to lose everything having coming this far. Before the demon could escape my sight I took flight and stood in front of his path.

"My sincere and humblest of apologies Gregorian, I may have spoken in ill repute but I do surely want your help, I just became slightly overwhelmed at the activities that I will have to engage in."

"Everything has a cost vampire, if you want something then you are required to do something."

"Yes I understand, however I cannot read the inscription on the scroll."

"Yes, which is why I will help you pronounce it, repeat after me"

Gregorian began speaking in foreign tongues and I tried my best to emulate.

"You must say it accurately and in one breath, not one word at a time and it can only be recited six times on the sixth hour. Any deviation and the entire plot will fail, you must say it like this:

"Inn'd Muhaa that tal ShayaaTeen, Issmah-lil ShayTaan anye yaQuun'lee"

As he spoke I quickly jotted down his words as phonetically as I possibly could into my journal. I only had one chance so I needed to do it properly.

"Is there anything else that I need to have or know?"

The twitch made its way into his hand.

"Finally, yes there is just one more thing, vampire."

Suddenly he vanished in front of my eyes, I looked around for him but couldn't find him. As I was unaware he crept up behind me and stabbed in my back hard with a blunt object. I shrieked in pain.

"Allow me to impart one final gift upon thee."

He was gritting his teeth as he continued to drive the object deeper into me as I struggled in pain. My blood began to boil inside the rotting carcass that was me; I was set alight from within and could feel a surge of energy running up my spine. In all my life and deadly animation I had never suffered this greatly before. The pain was immense and I lost consciousness due to it.

ASCENSION

I could feel the deep cutting of raw flesh under the sharpened edge of a sword. I could see blood trickling down the cheeks of the innocents as they watched the demise of their village. I could taste the death in the air and I knew I was in hell. All I could think of was how inappropriate actions could significantly determine the fate of others. Words like 'fairness' and 'equality' get tossed about by the self-righteous to impose a will on the weak. I was self-righteous as a vampire lord doing my Master's bidding but to what cost? In whose name did I kill the undeserving innocent? A price must be paid even by those in power that terrorise the innocent in a shroud of self-righteousness, I would need to pay the price. I woke from this thoughtful nightmare in a pool of coagulated blood.

It looked as though it had seeped out from my mouth whilst I was unconscious after being attacked from behind. I was groggy from the back pain and staggered slowly to my feet. My head felt heavy and my forehead was pulsating vigorously; I felt as though I was going to pass out again. I tried to soothe my suffering by massaging my head but as luck would have it I had changed ever so slightly again. It seemed as though the gift the demon had imparted on me was a small imprint of himself. Like him I now had horns coming out of my head, not as long but definable to say the least. Along with the horns a slight oozing of a green viscous material was coming from the tips, the liquid had no affect on me but as I wiped it on the ground it began to burn. An intriguing transformation that I hadn't truly appreciated until I saw a more definitive effect.

As I made my way to Lazarioss's kingdom I came to a savannah. I could see herds of animals grazing away contently on the pastures, I believe I may have come in between a male wildebeest and his offspring. The result of my unwilling action was instinctual anger from the animal, with its head down and horns primed the beast charged at me. As it caught me unawares I reacted quickly by cowering and anticipating the impact. What actually happened was the animal charged straight into the horns I had newly acquired, I heard a loud crunching of bone.

I opened my eyes to see what was going on, there dangling right in front of me was the animal's face. Somehow it had impaled itself onto the horns so I had to push it off me, as the beast hit the floor its skin began to shrivel and shrink. Most shocking was what happened next as its chest cavity erupted and blood shot out in great quantity. I did not truly understand the nature of these horns but the effects were undoubtedly fatal, naturally I assumed they were given to me in an endeavour against Alledantoro. If that was the case then I truly had a formidable and devastating option at my disposal, if he were close enough and the opportunity arose, I would charge at him like the wildebeest charged at me and he would disintegrate just like the unfortunate animal did. Despite this wonderful enhancement I was not about to let complacency take hold, I needed to consult with Lazarioss and ask for his aid. A deadly net was slowly being cast over Alledantoro, consisting of me, Gregorian and the knight's army.

As I arrived to the outskirts of the kingdom I found myself standing in front of an army outpost heavily guarded. An alarm was sounded and the walls of the encampment rapidly became full with reinforcements consisting of archers.

"You have come to the wrong place demon, you will not receive any mercy from us, to hell with you."

A volley of arrows was projected my way, I was surrounded by a small entourage of needle-like wood as the arrows stuck out of the ground all around me. The ones that had actually hit me, and done no damage whatsoever, decorated me like the spines on a porcupine. They all looked at me in disbelief as I calmly took the ones in me, out and threw them to the floor.

"I am here to seek an audience with Lord Lazarioss, it is of grave urgency."

"What business has an abomination got with the ruler of this land?"

"Impudent mortal do not test my patience, this slight spectacle is but a mere taste of my true devastation, if you wish to see what I could really do then continue to annoy me."

The knights began to look at each other, they all began to clamour around, I could hear metal clanking and bolts opening: the door was being raised. As I walked towards the opening I saw on the other side hundreds of knights gathered in one place behind one brave soul. A knight stood in front of me with his sword unsheathed.

"I am Dante, son of Ashcreena, captain of the northern realm's armies. You will tell me of your business with our ruler."

"Don't you recognise me Dante?"

"I don't believe we have met before."

"You gave me directions to the mountain keep of the vampires."

He quickly ripped off his helmet and took a long look at me whilst edging slightly closer to me, his faced dropped.

"It's you, the vampire that spared Lord Lazarioss."

"Yes, at last you recognise me."

"What in God's name has happened to you? You've become a hideous manifestation."

"Your words are heartening but I am here to accrue a favour that was made."

"Absolutely, Lord Lazarioss does not renege a pact once made, he will honour the pact he made with you.

Unfortunately he is away on urgent family business and has left me in charge. Ask of me what you will and I will assist to the best of my ability."

Even if Lazarioss wasn't there his subordinate at least could help.

"So be it, I require you to assemble your finest and strongest fighters to meet me in the northern hills in two days' time. The enemy is of epic proportions, this will truly be the fight of your life. We will attack him from all corners, you with your weapons and me with my powers."

"What exactly will we be fighting?"

"Something like me but magnified hundreds of times in strength and ability."

The knights became nervous but Dante had a glint in his eye.

"Very well sir, in two days we will assemble on the hills and be waiting to fight with you."

"And what of your Master, will he be joining us?"

"He may, I shall send word round to him immediately but it is doubtful he'll actually attend. Incidentally, why in two days sir?"

"I too have business to conclude before the fight."

"I have no doubt that this business of yours will alter your appearance once more."

"Your presumption is irrelevant. However, if you would be so kind, could you tell me of another thing?"

"By all means, ask away."

"I require impure blood, something that has been tainted. Would you know of such a place that I could obtain this kind of blood from?"

Confusion appeared on his face, "Forgive me vampire but we are all noble souls here. We all live righteous lives in the presence of almighty God."

"That is gratifying to know, still would you know of someone who does not live righteously thus condemning their souls in the eyes of your Lord?"

His eyes became cloudy with disgust, with a hand gesture he dismissed the knights to their stations. He walked hesitantly towards me and ushered me to come closer, as I leaned towards him he began whispering:

"There are those who defile themselves for petty gain, they use their own bodies as pleasure objects and ask for money. There is a town two miles to the east from here, at night these harridans come out and make a living. Go there and obtain what you seek."

The battlement gates shut with a thunderous thud and the bolts were applied forthwith. I looked towards the east and I took flight to this town.

I was under no illusion, I understood completely what he meant, I just took slight pleasure in seeing him describe such a person in discomfort. I came to a bustling town in the heart of the night, the streets were alive with laughter and zealous decadence. Truly this town had no sense of morals or duty, every corner was littered with indecency and sickness. I began to wonder how a noble soul such as Dante would know of such a place. I looked about the place for such a person he described so precisely. Standing in a doorway, vibrantly attracting men of low self-esteem to her, I saw my target, a harlot. She was wearing a low cut dress made with leather shoulder straps. Her clothing was red with blue frills going down the sides. Her face wasn't much to go by despite the copious amounts of make-up. I bided my time as I wanted to take her discreetly, time wore on and she started to walk quietly into a back alley.

At the end of this alleyway was an open sewage pipe that people used as a latrine, she began adjusting her clothes so she could relieve herself. As she squatted down I snatched her up and took flight to Sereigravo's mansion. Despite her virulent screaming nobody came to see the commotion, this was a sinful town that devoured itself, somewhat reminiscent of the world as a whole. I came to my former keep with the woman in tow, her perpetual screams had almost deafened me. As I stood in the main lobby I released my hold on her and she immediately made a beeline for the exit.

As her hand touched the doors handle I spoke, "Madam I urgently request that you do not open the door. I have brought you here for reasons beyond your understanding. If you dare defy me I swear you will be dead before your gizzards hit the floor!"

The threat was enough to make her silently abide by my ruling and she submissively came and stood next to me. I began surveying the keep looking for red lines as Gregorian had instructed me.

"Hey mister, what's going on? This isn't how we do business y'know."

Her words were like rotting offal to me.

"I know I ain't your kinda thing, a refined gentleman such as yourself."

"Depraved wench, I pray thee to look upon me

with your glistening eyes, do I look like anything you encountered before?"

She shook her deluded head.

"Then cease your insufferable verbal flatulence and let me think!"

I focused my gaze and found, to my surprise, red lines running across the top of the walls; they were razor thin but ran down the sides of the walls and into the corridors. I took hold of the woman and made my way through the corridors that had red lines, the lines got thicker but I came to a wall. It was hollow so I smashed through it. I made my way through the proceeding tunnel and saw a door was standing in front of me with an unusual lock. It was shaped like the silhouette of a hand with sharp pins at the tip of where every finger should be. My claws would not be appropriate but I knew what would work on this peculiar lock.

I forcibly took hold of her hand and pressed it against the curious indented lock. She shrieked in pain and began to cry as her blood opened the door. I peered past the door and an enormous staircase led down into a subterranean chamber, at the bottom I saw many symbols and ornaments decorating the interior of this consecrated room, especially one that looked liked interlaced triangles. I could feel the room pulsing with energy no doubt due to the activities practiced within. It was time for the ritual, I stood in front of a marble tiled floor that alternated in black and white shades. I could only assume that this was the transport module Gregorian had spoken of. It didn't look like it was going to move but then I was just going on blind instinct and instruction at this point.

I turned to the woman, "Give me your hand."

"No mister you already hurt me once, I don't mind if punters get a bit rough but this…"

I was in no mood for this so I took hold of her throat with my claws and brought her face close to mine.

"Give me your hand or die!"

She quickly adhered and I cut her palm with the tip of my claw. As she began nursing her hand, I held her forearm and began sprinkling her blood on the floor. She was in great discomfort but she was not my concern, once I felt enough blood had been shed I let her go and began walking on the marbled tiles.

She began running up the stairs, as she got halfway she turned around because she noticed I hadn't said anything or pursued her.

"What's the matter? Ain't you gonna tell me off again?"

I didn't reply and continued to walk towards the ceremonial pillars erected either side of the tiled floor.

"That's all you wanted a little bit of blood? You punters get more and more unusual everyday. Well I want something for my services at least."

"Take anything from this mansion you desire but go from here now!" She hastily ran up the stairs.

I sat down, legs crossed, between the two pillars on the tiled floor with my palms out. I waited until the sixth hour, once it came I closed my eyes and recited the prayer six times. As soon as I opened them I began to hear whispers, indistinct and random:

"Blood and bone…always let it be known…this is where the devil calls home…death and care always beware… children of the darkness never play fair."

A strong wind began sucking things up around me, I felt as though I was standing in the eye of the storm. My claws began to glow bright red and a surge of power shot up my spine. The marble floor began to glow and the tiles projected their shades to the ceiling of the room. The pillars began to rotate and glow bright gold. From the walls, repugnant spectres started seeping out as a parade all chanting the same hymn. Once again I had done something that I began to regret almost instantly. I looked around and saw the turmoil I had wrought in all my life, as though my existence had been a documented tale. This room had harboured some secrets in its time and it began to divulge them to me in imagery.

With the knowledge I found that through the practices and the power of the room and its symbols, I too had become illuminated and now possessed secrets from the dark ages past. It was time I faced the unknown precipice and I threw myself into the whimsical hands of fate. My armour-plated skin was pristine and glorious until it began to shrink and expand. I began to feel a strong gravitational pull within me and I exploded…

Whiteness upon whiteness with shades of grey, entities were able to walk within each other and then out the other side. The entire land was made up of what looked like wavy smoke, it swayed like the flame of a candle. I looked at my claws and could see them and through them. This entire plain of existence looked like a thin layer of smoke and through it I could see the universe. At will I could magnify my gaze on certain areas I had never seen before, distant worlds were accessible through this wondrous dimension. I could see the world I left behind, it was a large blue stone with hints of green mounted on white pivots. I was surging with a power that I had never felt before. As I tried to come to terms with where I was, beings from this existence continued to walk through me and themselves, as though I wasn't even there. It looked as though I had made it to the ether.

I tried to speak but no voice came out, I tried to stop one of the ethereal beings but they continued to pass through me. Slowly I began to sway side to side like them as they walked around. The buildings, the atmosphere, food, and bodies; literally everything looked as though it were made from wavy smoke. The only thing I could do was try to walk but even that became complicated, so I focused myself and then something strange started to happen. The atmosphere around me began to vibrate, so I stopped concentrating because I was fearful of something catastrophic. As soon as I did the atmosphere around me returned to normal. It was curious that my mental thoughts would have an effect on the surrounding environment. So I did an experiment: I began to focus once more to provoke the atmospheric reaction, as soon as it came I felt like running away. Then, amazingly, I had somehow transported to a completely different area, although generally it had the same consistency as the last place. So it seemed at this point the best way to get where you wanted to go was to will yourself there. With this idea in mind I focused my mind and the ethereal configuration sent me straight to Alledantoro.

It looked as though I had come at the right time, he and Gregorian were already fighting though not in a way I had ever seen before. Their bodies had merged and they were fighting each other, symbiotically bound to one another. Their features looked the same as they did in the normal world but in this realm they too swayed side to side. The fight was slow and strange, whatever it was that they were doing it looked as though Alledantoro was getting the better of the exchanges. A weakened Gregorian staggered back but Alledantoro put his head into Gregorian's chest and gnawed away at his heart. Gregorian slowly dissipated into nothingness, Alledantoro raised his gaze at me and began to smile. He raised his wavy arms at me and advanced forward, I wanted no part of this and wanted to be back in the normal world. As soon as he went to grab me I wanted Dante by my side so he could help me. Remarkably, I was back standing near him and his army next to some hills.

OUROBOROS

My desire to be back in the normal world had brought me back, though my actual appearance had changed slightly. Dante and his army looked like dwarves in front of me and my claws glistened handsomely in the daylight. They had assembled far ahead of schedule so I went to meet them. One knight shrieked in horror at the sight of me which alerted all the others to stand in an offensive posture. A knight pushed his way to the front; it was Dante who continuously looked more and more confused at the sight of me at every meeting.

"Noble vampire, is that you?"

"Yes it is me and I can actually say that I am happy to see you."

"It seems every time I see you a monumental change has overtaken your appearance. Have you completed your task with the unclean?"

"Yes with mind-boggling effects, that is irrelevant however. Why have you come here so early?"

They all began looking at each other slightly

confused and then erupted into hysterics.

"What are you talking about vampire? You said assemble in the hills in two days' time so here we are."

"I asked you two days ago?"

Dante nodded, I had lost two days whilst being in that realm, precious time that I needed to devise an attack strategy. Time does not adhere to the same scale in the ether, I began to feel a sense of urgency so I turned to Dante and quickly thought up a plan.

"Any minute now our enemy will be here, we must attack in a coordinated fashion."

"What do you mean any minute now? These tactical assaults take weeks to assemble and you're saying we have to fight at a moment's notice."

"You are a knight of this realm, if a threat presents itself then you must address it. If a fire consumes your home do you sit down and think of an exit strategy? No! You try to save your loved ones and leave. The same applies here, this foe is far more dangerous than any fire and he has the capacity and will to consume your lives." I announced to them all as if I were a general of the army. It actually felt like I was meant to do so as I had engaged them all in deep thought.

"Listen to me Dante, you and your men must muster the courage to fight, for if I fail then you will be the last hope your kingdom has. Before we allow it to come to that I ask you to fight as brothers, as one."

There was murmuring in the crowd but someone began to cheer in agreement, his enthusiasm sparked others to join and before long I had the approval of the entire force, even Dante, who was smiling in admiration.

"You should have been a general instead of the undead. In terms of strategy what do you suggest?"

"We cannot use stealth as he is far too developed to be deceived. We attack him head on, position your archers on the hills to send a volley at him if I am struck down. It will not hurt him but it should give your foot soldiers time to get to him and then you can unleash your deadly onslaught of heavily armoured warriors. In that time I should be able to reconvene the fight, I will with deal the majority of attacks. You are there in case things become too harrowing for me. I will try and keep him within those hills so that the archers are in range, I suggest you split your men into smaller contingents that can attack him wherever I fall."

Dante nodded in agreement. "You heard him men! Archers to the hill! Assemble the catapults at the base of those two hills, should give the fiend something to think about. Marcus, Quinn, Jeremiah and Salamore, assemble your teams and choose a hill! Today we go to war!!"

Dante roared at his army and they reciprocated. They began to scatter to their respective positions, Dante donned his helmet and nodded at me before doing the same. I walked slowly over to the middle of the hills that were now swarming with knights, as I looked upon them I knew that most would die before the day was out. Still I didn't feel like I had condemned them, rather I felt as though I had honoured them.

By giving them the opportunity to fight for their lives, I gave them a purpose, their faces were full of duty towards their kingdom and their country. They didn't care about the insurmountable odds they were about to face, they didn't care about dark rites and rituals or about secret orders trying to ensnare the world. They had much simpler thoughts on their minds, they wanted to protect their lands and their brothers in arms. I was truly humbled by their dutiful disposition.

I stood in the middle of the surrounding hills and roared into the air, "Alledantoro! I am ready, please will yourself here!"

A familiar wind manifested itself though not as powerful as before. The same kind of vortex I had seen before also appeared, and from that evil channel Alledantoro stepped out as regal as ever. He was the same height as me this time, I no longer felt as intimidated though I was not going to give foolish hope to myself. I was weary of what he could do considering the spectacle I was audience to in the ether.

"Heretic! You side with the opposition and my enemy, for what? To incur my displeasure and to look like an unholy abomination."

"My actions were my own, it is time we concluded matters."

"You may have ascended to the ether thus becoming a Sire but you are still no match for me, little one. You have only just emerged, I have been a Sire for over a century, what makes you think you even have the slightest of chances?"

"Look around you, I have assembled the finest and bravest souls in the land who, along with myself, are ready to do battle."

The old one wasn't intimidated at all by the threat we posed.

"Yes I saw them from the ether, I saw you as well at the mansion, doing something your father would have been proud of, unfortunately he wasn't able to watch. It's good that you've embraced your legacy and accepted the devil within yourself."

"Now who is speaking of heresy?"

He began to laugh at me, "You never have any idea about the things you get yourself into do you? I take it you don't know the meaning of the prayer you recited six times in six breaths on the sixth hour. You have invoked the pleasure of our Master."

I was at the point of no return, no matter what I had invoked the end was here.

"Be that as it may, it is of little consequence to me now, I care not for prayers to demonic entities as debased as you. I care not for secret covenants based on sickness and savagery. All I care about now is the reason I am here and that is to destroy you once and for all."

"So be it, little one."

We engaged each other in the middle, I had not counted on him being as slow as he was. His swipes and strikes were slow enough for me to evade with side steps. I took every opportunity to land a blow and evade any of his attacks. His slowness may have been due to the amount of time he spent in the ether; I started using different tactics while I could, with my telekinesis I raised him up and signalled the soldiers on the catapults, who sent a barrage of boulders that berated his face. They were doing minimal damage but it was still in my favour. He eventually escaped my hold by fading slightly into the ether. His power was developed to a point where he could do this at will. The boulders began to miss and my power became useless against him. He drifted over towards me and reanimated himself into this realm. As he fell on me and pinned me down he started scratching my face with those most heinous of claws; I was disorientated after a few strikes as his physical power was vastly superior to mine.

As I lay at his mercy, hundreds of arrows flew into the air; we could hear whistling in the air and as Alledantoro looked up to see what was going on the arrows landed. Some hit me in the face, arms and legs but most had covered the entire upper half of his body. He stood up off of me, slightly dazed and blinded from the ones that had landed on his face, I took this opportunity to land my strikes. I had whittled the arrows down to his face but he faded back into his ghostly form again. The arrows fell and he reanimated once more. Alledantoro now focused his attacks on the army, he ran up the hills and started swinging wildly with his claws, killing men by the rows in the formations. I tried to save them but every time I went to strike him Alledantoro utilised his fade manoeuvre then struck me down to the bottom of the hill. When most of the men lay dead he re-engaged me. I remembered that my telekinesis had other properties other than restriction. I did to him what I did to Raikarnor; as he took hold of me I concentrated on his face and a small explosion erupted there, he shrieked in agony and stumbled back.

"What kind of power is this? You would not have survived this long if you did not have this trickery."

"Well why don't you ask the accursed devil for assistance? Isn't he the despicable urchin you serve?"

He roared and we carried on fighting, slashing away at each other using our claws like swords. They would clash and sparks would fly, with a strong kick to the chest Alledantoro temporarily incapacitated me. I looked up whilst on the floor to see him prime his claws to deal a death blow. As he went in for the swipe a huge golden axe flew out of nowhere and stuck in his back, Alledantoro span round trying to pry it out. In the distance, standing on a hill, I saw him: Lazarioss had come to join the fight. With his sword unsheathed he charged at Alledantoro but was quickly swatted away, my opportunity had finally arrived, it was now or never. Alledantoro finally pulled the axe out and turned to face me, as he did I charged at him like a bull. He saw the danger and began to fade but it was too late. I had gored him in his chest, lifting him off his feet and throwing him away.

Alledantoro rolled on the floor in agony coughing and spurting blood, his body seized up with violent spasms. He looked at me wearily, I stared back into his eyes and his chest and abdomen erupted, spewing out black liquid that fell on the floor and burnt the ground.

*It is now finally over, Alledantoro now reduced to ash and my mission of self redemption has come to a close. So here I am now, sitting in front of a pile of ash with my story that has come full circle. True to his word Lazarioss served me well, allowing me the necessary diversion so I could finish it. I cannot see where he is, he must be lying amongst the countless dead bodies that are scattered all over these hills. I don't know what to think now, now that it is over. There is only one thing left to do now, as I promised to do when I set out on this mission. Everything is over: my life as a human, happiness with a family, any type of relationship with desired company and my purpose, everything is done. The only thing left for me to do now is to adorn this land with one more pile of ash, after everything that I have come to learn there is just one thing I would like to share with you. This illusory world that is full of pain will try to deceive you, do not let it devour you.

Take heed of what I say to you now, I am not Sire Crimson and I am not a scourge upon the world. I am Andross Ameliyo, a soul that has damned itself through selfishness and cowardice. I pray that I have regained some favour back, I conclude my wretched tale with a few simple verses,

"The moon stares back at me since I have no tune
I have scars on my soul just like the moon
With everything I had now gone
It is time for me to pass on."

IN HONOUR OF MY ELDER

'*One day you will be king, Lazarioss,*' a phrase my father would always say to me instead of a lullaby. I had always looked forward to it, but the circumstance by which it came fills me with dread.

If you ask me, even now, I don't think I will be able to give you an appropriate answer, in fact I believe that such an answer is non-existent. Nay, an answer is not required because faith is all I really need. I thank the Almighty for blessing me with talent and intelligence to recognise good within things that appear evil. As such, I knew I was onto something when I saw him, from the offset I did want to kill him, that much I confess, but after seeing him curiously turn from me I began to think *this vampire is no ordinary vampire, no normal fiend could better me let alone spare me.* As I spoke to him I felt as though I was speaking to an older brother, I was not under the influence of any hallucinogenic nor was I inebriated. I was fully aware of the situation and felt comfortable around him, which is what disturbed me so badly. The way I felt and the nagging thought that I had seen his face somewhere before.

After Dante told him where to find the mountain keep of the fiends my mind began racing with thoughts and questions. I needed answers that I could not get unless I retrieved some information. I gave Dante his orders and made my way back to the city walls. Inside the palace I summoned every scribe and learned man to my study quarters, I assigned them all with the duty to individually trawl through the family archives for something that could give me direction, anything that would tell me a little about this mysterious entity. If he had been here for over a century, some sort of record must be made, something as reckless as him must have raised some complaint. Hours passed and still I was no closer to finding out what I wanted. Days passed and the assembled men had become weary and tiresome. I dismissed them all so I could be alone with my thoughts. Then, remarkably, I had an epiphany: *this kingdom isn't the only one that has records but my revered aunty also has archives that date back nearly a hundred years or so.*

This aunty is special not because of who she is but because of where she is from. I am not necessarily of royal blood rather the elders of my family were ordained as royalty. She belongs to the old kingdom where our family dates back to when dignitaries owned land. They became popular and by consensus were voted to rule, thus making me heir to the throne. My beautiful aunty is bold and intelligent even at an elderly age, she always tells me that she got her spirit from her mother. I equipped and mounted my horse and made for my aunty's kingdom with great haste. I was welcomed with a fanfare and rows of cheering kinsmen and women and at the end of the red carpet leading to the castle she was standing there with a smile on her chaste face. I stood in front of her and was about to kneel when she stopped me, "There will be no need for such formalities my dear."

I embraced her lovingly and the whole crowd erupted with good cheer. We made our way into the palace and sat down in the main quarters. Tea was being served and our royal entourage were running around us in manic fashion. My aunty and I found this amusing but I was in a sense of emergency, she quickly dismissed them all and we began to chat.

"It has been such along time since you've been here Lazarioss, don't tell me you were too busy to meet with your aunty."

"Please excuse me, dear aunt, I would never want to displease you."

"Well it is heart warming to see you regardless, you can see that for yourself how everyone welcomed you, this is your kingdom too."

"Everyone keeps telling me that but I do not feel so. You are far more regal than I could ever be, your blood ties reach back to a time of beauty and elegance but also of pure heartache."

"Oh come on now, my dear boy, we've had this discussion; your blood is my blood, we both belong to the same family. I cannot bear children, which is why this kingdom lays dormant but my brother, your royal father, was an amazing man."

My beloved aunt loved my late father, his passing was harder for her than anyone else.

"I loved him and so did Mother, she is the one where it all started. This kingdom suffered a great loss in its inception during her time. The loss she suffered made me love my brother all the more," She said.

Our family's origins are steeped in tragedy.

"That is the reason I came, I am trying to ascertain some information on a character I believe I am familiar with, how I cannot say for sure but gut instinct tells me otherwise."

"I see, you have always been this way and that is why you will make a decent ruler, your ability to make the right choice. My kingdom and its contents are at your disposal Lord Lazarioss, my mother's diary entries are in the archives and you are most welcome to them. I shall assign some men to help you."

I rose off my chair and kissed her on her brow in gratitude. In the archives we unearthed countless material ranging from old encyclopaedias to outdated maps. We found globes, drawings and pieces of mouldy paper with indistinct scribbling on it.

One man shouted, "Eureka, Sire I have found something."

As he brought it over my heart began to race. It was indeed the diary of my grandmother, the matriarch of our kingdoms. I began reading through the different passages, they were full of what you would expect a young woman with a mournful heart to write about. I came to a few highly intriguing entries that I believed were what I had been looking for, I looked at one of the entries.

'What is left for me to do now but weep, everything is lost to me now. I may be in the care of my aunty but that is not who I want to be with. Life is so cruel to snatch everyone whom I have loved dearly as soon as we became happy. Father died, then sister died and just when I thought it couldn't get any worse brother disappears. Then I am taken into care and sit here day after day, lonely and dead.'

I skipped some passages to read others and found some insightful entries.

'So it seems due to our popularity there is a vote being cast that will solidify our names in history. I should be happy but then how can I be? I have lost all that I care about. What use is royalty if those that you love are not there to share it with you?'

I continued to read through the dilapidated book but realised that only the most recent entries would be the most relevant. I flicked through the diary towards the end and found a very powerful entry.

'I am still in a state of shock with regards to the events that have unfolded tonight. The castle is heavily fortified with hundreds of knights and barricades. There was anticipation of an attack tonight, though never in a million years would I have expected what actually happened. I sat on my bed crying uncontrollably, waiting for the inevitable as I could hear men savagely being killed outside my bedroom chambers. The killings stopped and I heard heavy footsteps, he smashed in and commanded me to follow him. His face, no matter how altered, still retained its beauty, my darling

sibling had returned finally to me...'

Reading this entry tears began to flow from my eyes, this was unprecedented documentation:

'...he didn't know how to react until I called out his name, I thank God almighty everyday that even though it was only for a little while he returned to me. In his arms I found the peace I had yearned for so many years. Despite being what he was, he held me the way he used to, in his arms with me sat on his lap. I was in utter bliss and the pain that had accumulated over all those years vanished. I informed the guard of who he was and they showed their appreciation. Suddenly another being much like him came in and they began to fight.

My beautiful sibling had a commemoration portrait made for him that hung above my bed, but it got broken in the encounter. Once the beast was dead he held me in his arm, then, to my utter grievance, he told me he was leaving. I tried to hold onto him but he told me to live my life and be happy, not like a shadow. I have decided I am going to take his advice, I will marry and my children will know of him, so will their children and the preceding generations will know of my brother who I was reunited with briefly but love more than life itself. His portrait may have been damaged but I will make sure future generations see it, encased in stone in the memorial gardens you will see him standing on a marble rock and you will recognise that he is my brother. This is my last entry as I have decided to grow up and not live in the past, with much love, Elizabeth Marioss.'

I felt a burning sensation inside my stomach. With haste I pushed people out of the way as I ran to the memorial gardens. Manically I searched high and low, looking at every statue and portrait of my kinsman that has passed. I was looking for one that resembled the description in Grandmother Elizabeth's diary. In the distance, hanging on a wall encased in stone, there was a picture of a man standing on a large marble stone. The inscription read:

'In loving memory of Andross Ameliyo, loving son, loving husband and loving brother to the house of Marioss. The light bearer of our family, may God rest his soul.'

I looked at the man, to my insurmountable grief it was him. The vampire, the fiend that had spared me was in actual fact my long lost kinsman. Suddenly a messenger ran to me as I sobbed silently.

"My Lord, captain Dante sends an urgent message, it reads: '*the noble fiend requests aid in two days at the northern hills,*' Orders?"

This was it, the time had come to repair what had split asunder. My family would be made whole again and the house of Marioss would rise from the ashes.

"Equip the fastest chariot and ready my battle armour. Today I bring back honour to my family."

"Yes, my Lord."

With great haste I made it to the northern hills after a day's ride. I found the place littered with bodies of fallen knights and in the distance I saw two giants fighting. I ran up one of the hills to get a better look, one of the giants kicked the other and the one that fell was the light bearer. My heart thumped very hard at my chest, he was in peril. I threw my axe with great accuracy and I hit his assailant, I drew my sword and advanced but was quickly dispatched. I woke heavily disorientated amidst the bodies and still had a sense of urgency to find him.

Finally I found him, sat down scribbling something in his journal in front of a pile of ash. I waited until he had finished. My eyes had longed to see him, all my life my family told tales of him and I wanted my eyes to get their fill of him after being deprived for so long. As he finished he stood up and was about to walk away until he saw me. He was much different now as he towered above but his face, despite being altered, was still the face of my kinsman.

"Alas Lazarioss you are here, no doubt to keep up your honour, you have my gratitude sir."

I choked with sorrow, my eyes filled with tears.

"What is this, Lazarioss? Surely you do not fear the sight of me."

I could not control myself any longer, "Andross Ameliyo!"

His face dropped and his eyes opened wider, "How do you know of such a name? Speak sir knight, I demand of thee!"

I confessed everything to him, "You are Andross Ameliyo, light bearer of the house of Marioss. You went missing over a century ago but Elizabeth remembered you in her heart. She wrote about you constantly."

He fell to his knees and lowered his head in disbelief, we were at eye level now and I walked over to him.

"We have a connection, we both felt it during our

first meeting. You are the rightful heir to the throne, we are your subjects, my lord, for you see Elizabeth Marioss is my grandmother."

He did not raise his gaze but merely sniffed the air, "The blood in your veins is the same as Liza's."

I was in a state of magnificent awe as I could not believe the opportunity God had blessed me with.

"She loved you dearly, our entire kingdom has mourned you for over a century and now you have returned. Light bearer, I beseech you, please say something."

He raised his face and tears were gushing from his eyes too, "Flesh of my flesh."

He held my face in his hands, "Just like Liza, I see her in your face my dear child. Her will and passion you are truly from her thus you are indeed my kinsman and I am Andross Ameliyo."

A chance reunion equal to no other in our realm's history.

"We are going to have a grand welcome, you will take your rightful place as ruler and our kingdom will rejoice in the presence of the king."

I took hold of his arm and tried to lead him. He would not move, instead he started to smile. I was slightly confused then Dante slowly crawled up to us and raised his head to say a few words, "Light bearer isn't it time you came home?"

Then he suddenly passed out due to his injuries.

I continued to urge him, "Light bearer, let's be on our way."

"You would have a vampire be king of your realm,

the same affliction that has plagued your people for years?"

"People won't care for what you are but who you are."

"You may or may not be aware but there are awesome forces at work in this world that will never let things get better for its inhabitants. What do you do against such odds?"

"They could have the dominion of the universe but so long as I believe in God I will always have the upper hand, they will have the illusory world, that's all."

He began to smile, "You have wisdom beyond your years but still you are naïve if you think everything is acceptable. A burden must be carried by me resulting from my actions and here be the results."

I was confused, "Grant me one favour," he said.

"You have but to ask."

"When you see the world, tell it about me."

Before I could say another word he began to use his invisible lifting power against me. He tore off his horns and looked upon me with a loving smile as I was suspended in mid air, "Goodbye sweet prince, I'll send Liza your love."

Before I could protest he launched me away and I caught a slight glimpse of him about to stab himself in the chest. I landed far away and on my head, which knocked me unconscious. I awoke with many knights rallying around giving aid to those in need and carrying the dead on wagons. I ran to see what my heart was dreading. I saw the pile of ash had spread and he was no longer there; I could not fathom the need to do such a deed after being reunited with a family member. My immutable sorrow took hold and I buried my face in the ash that I believed to be my fallen comrade. There amidst the ruin I found his writings and after reading them realised the heavy heart he carried with him.

*Whoever you are reading this, realise that even if you are the embodiment of evil or its agent, you have the capacity to redeem yourself in the eyes of the Lord. I care not for orders or covenants but I care for my soul; be the best you can be and fight injustice and tyranny wherever you can find it in all its guises.

I, King Lazarioss, submit to you *The Memoirs of the Damned*.